G000269502

Pip in Pompeii

Pip in Pompeii

KATE PROCTOR

This is a work of fiction. Names, characters, places, and incidents either are the product of the author's imagination or are used fictitiously. Any resemblance to actual persons, living or dead, events, or locales is entirely coincidental.

Copyright © 2022 by Kate Proctor

All rights reserved. No part of this book may be reproduced or used in any manner without written permission of the copyright owner except for the use of quotations in a book review. For more information, address: kateproctorauthor@yahoo.com

First paperback edition 2022

Illustrations by Freya Lowy Clark

ISBN 978-1-80227-357-1 (paperback)
ISBN 978-1-80227-356-4 (ebook)

Published by PublishingPush.com

Typeset using Atomik ePublisher from Easypress Technologies

For my mum

One

The dead magpie hung in the water, shining purple and green like a petrol spill. Toothless poked it with a stick, sending the dead bird to the bottom of the murky canal and ripples fanning away towards the nesting coots over by the far bank.

Pip shuddered. She didn't like getting in when there were dead animals around. She had swum around a dead fox once. It had mould for fur and was so bloated she was afraid it would burst.

"Get in, Pip. I want at least a kilo by dinner time and do not, I REPEAT, do not let anybody see you, especially that nosy parker Sergeant Bunn. Do you understand?" Toothless thrust a string bag at her then turned to go home, inching her flabby frame along the bank like a slug.

Once the old woman was out of sight, Pip crouched down to sit at the water's edge. A big grey cloud covered the feeble sun and spots of rain were starting to fall onto her shoulders. A tiny pink and whiskered nose emerged from Pip's pocket and sniffed the air.

"It's the same as usual, Mrs Higgins, cold and damp." She gently took the mouse from her pocket and placed her on the canal bank. "Keep a look out, would you? I'll get into terrible trouble if Sergeant Bunn catches me. He keeps asking why I'm not at school. I wish I WAS at school," she said.

She slipped silently into the water. The canal wasn't deep. She had soon sunk to the bottom to begin her search. She felt among the stones for bits of metal to put into her bag. The stones were slippery with slimy weeds and the water thick with muck and sludge.

Pip was hungry and determined to find enough scrap metal to put

1

Toothless in a good mood. When Toothless was in a good mood, she was more generous with her food. Yesterday's haul had been poor; a few drinks cans and a rusty old trowel. Last night's meal had matched her meagre findings.

She passed her hands over the stones. She felt for the sharp rim of a tin or the bevelled edge of a coin. Something shiny towards the middle of the canal caught her eye and she swam over, pushing herself down so she was close enough to grab it.

With three sharp tugs, she freed the battered old teapot from the silt and placed it in the string bag along with the claw hammer and bent fork she had found earlier.

Pip surfaced to come up for air. She was good at holding her breath. Once, when pulling a rusty shopping trolley from between two concrete slabs, she had held her breath for two whole minutes.

She found a rock to cling to and looked back at the bank where she had left Mrs Higgins. The mouse was jumping up and down frantically. The wind caught the mouse's frenzied squeaks, carrying them to Pip;

"The coots! The coots!"

Looking around, Pip realised that she was very near the far bank where the coots were nesting. It was too late. She had swum too far. The coots began to shriek.

One charged at Pip, head down, his clawed feet propelling him through the water, but, just in time, Pip launched herself away from the angry bird. Narrowly missing a sharp peck on the nose, she swam quickly to the opposite bank.

"Phew! That was close," she panted to the mouse. She levered herself out and found her clothes that she had left neatly folded and hidden by the wall, amongst the nettles. She pulled them on and offered her arm to Mrs Higgins who scuttled up and settled in her hair.

The bag clanked reassuringly as Pip picked it up and tossed it over her shoulder.

"There MUST be more than a kilo in there," she said to the mouse hopefully. "Tonight, we will dine like kings." She expanded her chest and patted her tummy.

"I wouldn't count on it," squeaked her friend. "You know how mean Toothless is. Still, things won't be like this for much longer. There's a change in the air, young Pip, you mark my words."

The mouse had swung down Pip's forehead on a strand of hair and was dangling above the bridge of her nose, making her go cross-eyed.

"Why? What do you mean?"

"Patience, my dear, patience," she squeaked before grasping the hair strand like a rope and hauling herself back into the damp mound on top of Pip's head.

Pip wasn't in the mood for intrigue. She felt sad. Tomorrow she was going to be thirteen, although she was sure nobody would have remembered. Even Mrs Higgins hadn't mentioned it.

Home wasn't far and she was glad she was returning with a full bag for once. She pushed open the iron gates, noticing that the sign declaring 'Toothless & Ruthless Recycling Partnership' had lost a nail and was hanging awkwardly, revealing the original 'Regency House' sign behind it.

'I suppose I'll have to fix that in the morning,' she thought glumly to herself.

Without looking up, Pip could feel the big dark house looming over her, sucking what little light was left from the atmosphere. She walked in its shadow through the cluttered yard and round to the back door, letting herself in with her key.

Toothless was sitting by the fire in the otherwise gloomy kitchen, the bulk of her great carcass resting on an armchair. She was stuffing great dollops of syrupy sponge pudding into her mouth.

Her monstrous legs were propped up by two footstools. Nurse Bladderwash was applying a poultice. A cigarette hung from the corner of the nurse's mouth and smatterings of ash fell onto the bandages as she wound them around Toothless' sagging knees.

"What do you have for me, child?" demanded Toothless through a mouthful of pudding. "Put it on the table. Let me see."

Pip emptied her bag and the things she had collected fell onto the grooved and dented wood of the old kitchen table; the teapot, the hammer and the fork. Pip stood back proudly.

Toothless tutted, placed her bowl on her big tummy and thrummed her free hand slowly on the arm of her chair.

"Do you call that a day's work, you idle specimen? I was cursed the day I took pity on you and raised you as my own, Pip." Toothless turned to her scrawny friend.

"Do you remember that day, Bladderwash? Not even a year old and her mother abandoned her to go galivanting around the world." Bladderwash listened intently, pulling on a thin cigarette. She nodded. Toothless went on;

"THAT'S what happens when you try and help someone; they leave you in the lurch. Turned up on my doorstep the size of a house she did, asking me if I could 'put her up' for a while." Toothless made circling gestures with her hands. "Said we were family, I dunno, seventh cousin twice removed or something silly like that. Said she was Norman's daughter. Do you remember him, Bladderwash? Thin as a rake, always had moist hands. I think he was a librarian before they shut all the libraries and he begged ME for a job, always in a cardie anyway…" Bladderwash shook her head and tutted.

"Oh, you MUST remember Norman. It was him who had the terrible accident with the smelting machine. They tried to blame me. The cheek of it. Health and safety regulations or some such rubbish."

Toothless paused to shovel more pudding into her grinning mouth, then chomped for a while, then swallowed. She turned to Pip;

"So, she swanned off just before your first birthday, your mother, and left me to raise her first-born. Only the good Lord knows where she is now. Probably sipping cocktails somewhere. Who knows? And you insult me with THIS? You're a lazy good-for-nothing. How much do you think these petty trifles will fetch at auction? Hmm…? Not much, I can tell you… Nothing more than dry bread for you tonight, my girl. Go on, get out of my sight!"

Bladderwash looked blankly into the fire as Toothless bent to rummage in the bin beside her chair. She found a chunk of grotty bread to hurl at Pip who deftly caught it and darted out of the kitchen.

4

She knew better than to stay and argue and started the long climb up the creaking staircase to her bedroom in the attic.

Deflated, she trudged up the five flights of stairs. The house had once been grand but now the paint had faded, and wallpaper hung sadly in dusty shreds. In near darkness, Pip felt for the ladder that would lead her to her room. With cold hands, she clung tightly to the rungs until, launching herself through the small square hatch at the top, she flung herself onto her tiny mattress.

"Hey! Careful!" said Mrs Higgins, her voice a muffled squeak in the tangle of Pip's hair. "I'll be squashed flat."

"Oh, sorry!" Pip said laughing. She sat up, reached into her hair and untangled her friend. She placed her on her bedside table. She scrabbled around her bed for a box of matches and lit a candle.

The spluttering flame disturbed the group of bats that had been resting on a low beam. They took off and flapped upwards, making Pip jump.

"Ah, goodnight, ladies," Mrs Higgins shouted into the eaves. "They're really only mice with wings, you know."

They both looked up, their eyes following the flutter up to the eaves of the roof.

"I'm hungry," Pip said, looking back down at the lump of bread in her hand.

"Ah yes; I have something for you. Save that for the birds." She nipped into the bedside table drawer, emerging a few moments later with the edge of a paper bag in her teeth. She pulled and pulled until she'd almost freed it from the drawer.

"Help me, will you? I stole this from the pantry earlier; tuck in."

Pip took the bag from her, put in her hand and pulled out a plump chocolate muffin.

"How did you manage to haul this up all the stairs?"

"Ah, the girls gave me a hand," Mrs Higgins said, looking up to where the bats were roosting. "I was saving it for tomorrow. It's a birthday cake of sorts but it's better that you have it now since you're hungry."

"Oh," said Pip, brushing crumbs from her chin. "You remembered; thank you."

"Of course I remembered, you silly sausage. I've been looking forward to your birthday for a very long time. It's a REAL coming of age… thirteen."

"I wish my mum was here," said Pip reaching under her pillow for a crumpled photograph. She smoothed it out on her knee. "I have her eyes, I think. Tell me again, what was she like?"

Mrs Higgins broke off a large crumb of Pip's muffin, put it in her mouth, chewed and swallowed.

"What IS she like do you mean? She is adorable. She is kind and clever and funny and she loves you very much."

"Then why did she leave me with Toothless?" Pip asked.

"She had to. She thought she was doing the right thing. She didn't know she wouldn't be able to get back, that's all. You have to believe that. Don't listen to what Toothless says. She's nasty and tells lies."

"She keeps saying she abandoned me."

"Look, it will all become clear soon enough. I promised your mum I'd keep an eye on you in her absence and I've done the best I can. She was a good friend to me. I miss Carrie too."

Pip yawned and rubbed her eyes.

"You need some sleep, Pip; big day tomorrow," Mrs Higgins said, cleaning crumbs from her whiskers. "Blow out that candle and snuggle down, that's a girl." As soon as Pip's head touched the pillow, she was fast asleep. Mrs Higgins crept away. She scrambled down the ladder, climbed the stair railing and slid down the huge, once-shiny mahogany banister. She then squeezed under the crack of the kitchen door.

"Damn and blast, that wretched mouse is back again, Bladderwash. I KNOW it was her who stole one of my muffins yesterday. Where's that lazy moggy? Silas! Silas! Get that blasted mouse," said Toothless from her armchair.

"Now, now. You shouldn't really be encouraging the cat to kill your sister; you know what would happen if he did," said Bladderwash as she puffed out a perfect smoke ring. She was standing at the fire, warming her knees. Bladderwash always felt cold.

"A mouse for a sister; who would have thought? Mind you, that's what happens when rules are broken."

Silas the cat lifted his head from the rug by the hearth and let it fall again, ignoring Mrs Higgins as she darted past to hide behind the fire utensils. He was too old for chasing mice. His head dropped back onto the rug to join his body in a deep, feline sleep.

The two women soon forgot about Mrs Higgins. Their conversation turned to Pip;

"You might as well tell her the truth, Toothless. The truth about the canal; the secrets it hides and the riches it holds." Bladderwash paused to take a drag of her cigarette; "It's not as if she's earning her keep as a mud lark. She's thirteen tomorrow. Old enough to be put to proper use, if you ask me."

Toothless thought hard. "I'm not sure she's ready. Look what happened to that stupid mother of hers. She wasn't up to the job, so I don't have much faith in her offspring."

"If you don't get her out of the way and earning a decent crust, that sticky-beaked policeman is going to throw his oar in. Pip has started asking questions. She's at that age now. One careless word from her about Carrie disappearing and he'll get the authorities involved. You mark my words."

"You have a point, my friend," Toothless said, scratching her stubbly chin. "Where should we send her to? Do you think she'd manage Russia in 1917? I've always fancied Empress Alexandra's jewels. Or what about 1922 to pinch Tutankhamun's mask?"

"It's a pity you got too fat to squeeze through the tunnel or you could go yourself. I'll never forget the time you were nearly crushed to death by one of Hannibal's elephants. Do you remember?"

"How could I forget, you daft woman? And anyway, I'm too long in the tooth. Why worry about that when I have someone else to go for me?"

"Whatever happens, you mustn't allow her to get her mitts on the key to Pompeii. If she finds half-witted Carrie there and brings her home, we can say goodbye to all this. We'll end up in clink," said Bladderwash shivering at the idea of a cold gaol cell.

"Nothing to fear there, my dear Bladderwash," Toothless delved into her dinner-stained smock and pulled out a large, black iron key hanging on a grubby piece of string around her neck. "See this here? THIS is the key to Pompeii and I never take it off, even at night. It's as safe as houses." She scratched her chin again. "It's decided then. I'll have a word with her when she gets back from the canal tomorrow evening."

"At last," said Bladderwash. "It's about time we saw some luxury around here again. Let's return the old house to its former glory and live like the glamour girls we used to be."

"Oh please, spare me the thought of you in sequins. It will put me off my supper," Toothless moaned.

Mrs Higgins was still hiding behind the hearth brush. Now that she knew where Toothless was hiding the key to Pompeii, she could see Pip's adventure coming to life at last. She peered through the bristles. When Bladderwash had sat down to knit and Toothless had begun to doze, she shot across the hearth past Silas, dashed under the door crack, sped up the stairs and under the hatch into the attic. She tiptoed over Pip's blankets and made a comfy nest for herself in her hair. There she rested but didn't close her eyes.

Two

When Pip awoke, she was alone. She sighed, remembering that it was her birthday. She got up, dressed and slipped down the ladder onto the landing. She jumped onto the banister and slid all the way to the bottom, Toothless' snores becoming louder as she made her descent.

"Ah, good morning, Pip, and happy birthday." Mrs Higgins was cleaning her whiskers on the bottom step.

"Thank you… I suppose…, I nearly trod on you." Pip was cross.

"Hey, don't be like that. There's something I need to talk to you about, but it must wait until we're away from this house. Pop me into your pocket. Toothless must think it's business as usual today."

Pip scooped up her friend, letting her fall gently into the front pocket of her jeans. She turned the large brass knob on the kitchen door and let herself in. Last night's fire was still smouldering in the grate and Toothless' armchair held nothing but grubby, sagging upholstery.

She then made her way over to the pantry. She turned the key in the lock and went inside. The pantry was almost as big as the kitchen. Shelves brimming with food lined the walls from the bottom to the top. The food in the pantry made its way into Pip's dreams almost every night. Her eyes passed longingly over the pudding bowls, topped with muslin, waiting to be steamed. She could smell the plump raisins and candied peel hidden inside.

She banged her head on a giant ham hanging from a hook on the ceiling as she squeezed past the wobbly jellies and crusty apple pies. She collected everything she needed for Toothless' breakfast and ticked off every item against those listed in the provisions book. Toothless didn't trust Pip not to steal her precious food.

She carried everything into the kitchen and locked the pantry door. Pip wasn't enjoying her thirteenth birthday much. To her, it was just another boring day of drudgery.

She started to cook. Into a huge iron frying pan went some eggs, sausages, bacon, mushrooms and tomatoes. She wondered if her mum was eating breakfast right now. A salty tear plopped onto the pan, making the butter spit.

As she dished out the breakfast, Toothless appeared at the door, breathing heavily. She sat down at the table and held her cutlery expectantly. Toothless didn't speak in the mornings until she had been fed. Pip carried her brimming plate over and placed it in front of her.

Not wanting to witness the ugly spectacle of Toothless eating, Pip turned away to put on her anorak, gulping down some toast as she did so. She collected another key from a hook by the door.

"DO NOT LET ANYONE CATCH YOU IN THE CANAL," Toothless bellowed suddenly, "AND BE BACK EARLY; I NEED TO SPEAK TO YOU ABOUT SOMETHING."

'So many people want to speak to me today', Pip mused to herself. 'Maybe they are all planning a surprise party', but she didn't really think they were.

"Oh, and get that sign nailed back up. PLEASE try and earn your keep today." Toothless sprayed egg down her front as she shouted.

Pip closed the door gently as she left and before heading to the canal, crossed the yard to collect the recycling, another of her daily chores.

The cottage had been built for the canal's lock keeper. Pip unlocked the front door, pushed it open and lit a candle on a shelf in the hall. The flame lit up a rack of thirteen keys that was nailed to the wall. Each key was made of cast iron and painted black, and each fitted one of the thirteen locks along the canal.

Pip reached for a key, unhooked it and placed it on her palm. She felt the cool of the metal against her skin. The key was so large, her palm couldn't contain it. She put it back on the rack.

"No time for daydreaming," Mrs Higgins piped up, scampering up Pip's arm to rest on her shoulder.

Pip walked past her old bedroom. The door was ajar, and she caught a glimpse of the faded teddy bear paper on the walls. Mrs Higgins noticed her looking at it and sighing.

"I helped your mum put that up, you know, although, I was probably more of a hindrance. I fell into the paste pot."

"Yes, I know. You've told me that story a thousand times."

"Hey, I'm only trying to cheer you up."

"Well, I'd rather not think about my mum right now, if that's alright." Mrs Higgins took the hint and clambered back down into Pip's jeans pocket.

Pip pushed on to the back of the cottage, into the kitchen which was now full of tin cans, plastic bottles and newspaper. Toothless had made four holes in the outside wall of the cottage which now lined the pavement of the road leading to the supermarket. A sign had been nailed onto the cottage wall stating;

"BE GREEN. MINIMISE YOUR CARBON FOOTPRINT. BE KIND TO THE PLANET. RECYCLE YOUR RUBBISH HERE. (Please separate plastic, metal and glass and paper.) Thank you."

Little did people know that Toothless was only interested in the glass and the metal. The rest she threw away.

Pip collected up all the recycling from the floor and put it into the appropriate bags; those for saving and selling and those for throwing away. She hauled the bags from the cottage, locked the door, dragged them to the other end of the yard and finally set off for the canal.

Head down, Pip dug her hands into her anorak pockets and stamped along the towpath. She stopped briefly to look at a heron perched on one leg on the opposite bank, then plodded on towards the tunnel. When she emerged, she noticed the sun shining weakly from behind a cloud. By the time she had gone through the last tunnel, she looked up to see that the sun had nudged the clouds away. She had reached her diving spot. Mrs Higgins scampered up her arm; "Sit down, Pip. We need to talk. Not here though, behind that bush," she said pointing a pink paw towards some shrubbery by the railings. Pip did as she was told, laying her anorak over the grass that was still damp with morning dew.

"Is this going to take long?" The morning sun hadn't brightened her mood.

"Well…" the mouse mused, "I'll try and keep it short, but it certainly won't be simple." She climbed up Pip's bent leg and settled on her knee. Pip looked directly at her, exhaled loudly then looked away.

"So… where to begin?" the mouse said, scratching her chin.

"At the beginning?" Pip had begun to make circles in the soil with a piece of twig.

"Your mum, Carrie…" Pip straightened suddenly and stared at her friend. Mrs Higgins went on;

"Yes, Carrie, your mum… it all began just over thirteen years ago. She was expecting you and had fallen on hard times after your father disappeared. She was all alone in the world but remembered her cousin Toothless up by the canal in Regency House. She knew Toothless ran some sort of business and came to her asking for help."

Pip started to fidget.

"But why…?" she began.

"Just LISTEN," the mouse interrupted her. "Toothless was very kind at first. She welcomed Carrie with open arms. She settled her into the lock keeper's cottage where she made a nice little nest for herself. Little did Carrie know there was a price to pay. Rather a huge price, actually." Pip's eyes were as wide as saucers.

"Go on…"

"Well… You were born, and we all made a big fuss of you; even Toothless seemed to melt a little. Funny little thing you were. Chattering all the time. You were talking before you were ten months old.

ANYWAY, just before your first birthday, Toothless turned up at the cottage. Carrie opened the door. She held you with one arm, balancing you on her hip. She was no doubt smiling and you were probably giggling about something.

She invited Toothless in and they sat down in the kitchen. I was hiding behind the pepper pot, listening to every word.

'Nothing in life is free' she said to your mum. 'Everything comes with a price. You've spent too long here free-loading, taking advantage of my good nature.'

That sort of thing, you know. I have to say, Carrie was shocked and on the verge of tears. Before she could tell Toothless she had nowhere else to go, the old woman stopped her. 'There is a way out, of course,' she said. 'If you can just do one little job for me, you can stay here as long as you like. It just means a short trip away from Pip. It shouldn't take more than a day or two and you'll be back before her first birthday. We'll all be waiting here for you and we'll have a cake and balloons. Everything to make a happy first birthday party for young Pip.'

Your mum was beside herself with worry at first. She'd not spent more than half an hour away from you before but with the threat of being turfed out of your home hanging over her, she told Toothless to carry on."

Mrs Higgins stopped suddenly. They both heard a cheery whistle approaching from the towpath.

"Oh no," Pip said. "That sounds like Sergeant Bunn."

The whistling became louder. Pip made herself small, hugging her knees into her chest. Suddenly, Lester, Sergeant Bunn's police dog, came bounding round the hedge. He was thrilled to see Pip and wagged his tail furiously.

"No, Lester, stop it," Pip pleaded quietly as he licked her face, making her laugh. They heard a sharper whistle from the path.

"Come on, boy. What are you doing messing around in the bushes? Get out of there. I have to get to the bakery before they sell the tastiest treats. Come on… Good lad."

Pip patted Lester's head then pushed him back around the bush.

"Phew," she whispered. "That was close." Mrs Higgins waited until the policeman's happy whistle became faint, and she climbed back onto Pip's knee to resume her story.

"Where was I? Oh yes…

'Here's the thing,' Toothless said. 'This here canal was built a very long time ago. A marvellous piece of engineering, wouldn't you agree?'

she asked your mum, though poor Carrie was baffled. 'The architect, very clever man, Nash was his name. He was my great- great-great-great-great-grandfather,' she said. 'As well as designing all of the thirteen locks, he also designed a very clever little device. The very clever little device that can save your bacon. Just next to the thirteenth lock, Nash built a time portal!' Well, your mum's jaw hit the floor at this point, as has yours, I see." Mrs Higgins paused.

"Go on, I want to hear."

"So Toothless went on to explain how the grid on the portal has a dial. The dial can be turned to a year of your choosing, but there is also a keyhole. The dial selects the time, but the key determines the place."

"So where did my mum go?" Pip asked.

"Toothless gave your mum the key to Pompeii. She made her go back there just before the eruption of the volcano in AD79. You know, Vesuvius?"

"Yes, I know all about Pompeii and Vesuvius, but wasn't that awfully dangerous?"

"Yes, of course it was, but Toothless is greedy and wanted your mum to collect valuables from the people of Pompeii before the eruption to bring back here so she could sell them. She always said people are very easily separated from their wealth in times of disaster."

"Wow. That really is evil; poor Mum."

"When Toothless was a young woman, she used to travel back in time herself. She went with Bladderwash. They made a very good living out of it, I can tell you. Sadly for her, she got too, 'large', shall we say? Too large to fit through the tunnel. She made me go once and that was catastrophic for me."

"Is that really a job for a mouse?"

"I haven't always been a mouse, my dear girl. I was once known as Harriet Nash. I'm her sister."

"Whose sister?" Pip scratched her head.

"Toothless' sister," said the mouse. She went on, "Don't you think it's a little bit odd that I can talk?"

"Everything in my life is a little bit odd. What happened to you?"

14

"I fell victim to one of the most devastating rules of the canal portal. You must NEVER EVER warn anyone of their impending doom. You can never tell people of the tragedy that's about to befall them. If you do, you'll be turned into a creature: the creature you happen to be closest to at the time the beans spill…"

"Is that what you did?"

"You've read about the Great Fire of London?"

"Yes, 1666."

"That's right, well, off I went in 1666 with the strict instruction to steal Samuel Pepys's diaries."

"You warned people about the fire?"

"I did. I organised a mass evacuation. Have you never wondered why only one person died in that fire? So, here I am, a mouse. They do say that in London, you're never further than a metre away from a mouse or a rat. I wonder, would I have fared better as a rat? A much-maligned creature, you know? Some of the kindest people, well, animals, I've known have been rats. Anyway, I digress, there's more to tell you about your mum.

Obviously, she was terrified of leaving you behind but Toothless assured her that you'd be very well taken care of and that she wouldn't be gone for long. In fact, time travel takes no time at all – you'll see."

"What do you mean, I'll see?" Pip looked perplexed.

"Carrie and I made a pact. She made me promise that if she didn't return, I would keep the story secret. I wasn't allowed to mention her ill-fated trip until your coming of age. Thirteen was the age we agreed on."

"I see," said Pip, but really she didn't.

"And then, after your thirteenth birthday, you'd rescue her from Pompeii so you could be reunited."

"What? Me? By myself? How can I possibly rescue her?" The colour drained from Pip's face.

"I have faith in you, my dear girl, and anyway, Toothless has other plans for you. She wants to send you somewhere else, somewhere very far away from Pompeii."

"Would you come with me?"

"No, Pip. My time-travelling days are well and truly over. I will only slow you down. Not only am I a mouse, but I'm quite an old mouse. It's time for you to stand on your own two feet and break away from this place. Then, you can start living a normal life, hopefully with Carrie. I will be here waiting for you. You can do it, Pip."

"I miss my mum." Pip looked up into the sky.

"Yes, my dear girl, and now is your chance to find her and bring her home. Look sharp though, this needs to seem like a normal day to Toothless. She is going to talk to you about her plans later. She mustn't find out about Pompeii. You'd better jump in the canal and collect some scrap for her."

Pip didn't know what to think. Her head seemed to be twirling on its axis. She undressed and put on her swimming costume. She walked to the edge of the canal and slipped silently into the water.

Three

"So, why are you called Mrs Higgins and not Miss Nash?"

Having collected a length of lead piping and a beaten old watering can, Pip swam back to her friend with the question.

"Ah, you have Ralph to blame for that; Ralph Higgins. I met him in the old coach house. He was a field mouse really, but we got on very well."

Pip levered herself up onto the lower gate of the thirteenth lock. She sat on the wooden arm.

"What happened to him?"

"Slashed to pieces by Silas, I'm afraid. I was left alone with seven babies to look after. I think that's why I had so much sympathy for your mum. It's not easy being a single parent. Not easy at all."

"And your babies, what happened to them?"

"I lost one to the broom, another two to Silas, and one went the cruellest way possible - a sticky paper trap. I never got over that one."

"And the other three?" Pip's shoulders were starting to dry off in the sun.

"Oliver was taken by a tawny owl and Susan ate poison. Larry was the only one who survived. He moved to Hackney and we lost touch." "That's so sad."

"Well, that's life when you're a mouse, I'm afraid, so you'd better keep your trap shut in Pompeii."

"Yes… about that…"

"See over there by the coots' nests?" Mrs Higgins interrupted. "That's where you'll find the time portal, but don't worry, the coots will be asleep when you make your little trip."

"But how will…?" Pip began again.

"It will all become clear in good time. Toothless aims to send you to Russia, I think. You must play along until we steal the key to Pompeii. We'll do that tonight."

Pip collected up everything she'd found in the canal and put it all in her string bag. She lowered herself back into the water, slinging the bag over her shoulder. She cupped Mrs Higgins in her other hand, propelling herself backwards to the canal bank with her legs. She looked straight into her friend's eyes;

"Do you really think I have what it takes? To rescue her?"

"Yes, I do, I really do," said the mouse, who was cleaning her whiskers with her paws.

A familiar whistle interrupted their conversation. There was Sergeant Bunn, tubby and awkward in his tight blue uniform. Mrs Higgins darted into Pip's hair while Pip tried to make herself small with her back against the canal bank, but it was too late. She had been seen.

"Ah, hello, Pip, there you are. How is the home-schooling going? No lessons today?"

Pip's heart sank. She knew she was going to be in trouble when she got home. She thought quickly;

"Physical education, Sergeant Bunn. I'm having a swimming lesson, although Toothless can't leave the house very easily because of her knees, so I came by myself. I've already swum twenty widths."

"Hm…," he said, thinking hard as he dusted cake crumbs from his beard. "What are those things you've gathered?" He had noticed Pip's bag of metal, "I hope Toothless hasn't put you to work out here in the filthy canal. That would be highly illegal."

"Oh no, no, not at all." Pip heaved herself onto her elbows, then deftly turned to sit on the edge of the canal. Lester rushed over wagging his tail. He licked Pip's face until she started to laugh. She placed her string bag at the policeman's feet. "I'm just doing a bit of tidying up. A cleaner canal is easier to swim in." She patted Lester.

Sergeant Bunn was still deep in thought;

"Have you had breakfast?"

"Of course." Pip's stomach growled noisily. The policeman pondered this as he carefully lifted off his tall, dark blue hat. Pip's eyes grew and her mouth began to water when she saw what he had been hiding underneath. There were thirteen, she counted them, thirteen sugar doughnuts glinting in the sunshine.

"Baker's dozen," he said. He was embarrassed; "In case I lose one." He lifted the plumpest doughnut from the top of the pile. He was careful not to let any of the others fall. He looked at it and sighed. He brought it to his face and sniffed it. Pip watched a globule of raspberry jam ooze from a hole in its top. It dribbled out and landed on Lester's nose with a plop.

"Well, all the same, Pip, I think you should have this. It will do you good after all your exercise. I still have twelve left. That should tide me over until lunchtime."

Pip gratefully took the doughnut from the policeman's outstretched hand.

"Thank you, Sergeant Bunn," she mumbled through a mouthful of tasty, sugary, gooey dough. Distracted by the delicious treat, she didn't notice the policeman put his hat back on and pick up her string bag. He tucked it under his arm and said goodbye with Lester dancing at his heels.

"Well, that was lovely." Pip wet her finger and rubbed raspberry jam from her chin. She jumped to her feet, her eyes scanning the canal bank for her bag of metal.

"Don't bother. Sergeant Bunn took it with him. He'll be expressing his concerns about you to Toothless RIGHT now." Mrs Higgins jumped onto Pip's shoulder. She shook herself dry.

"That's the end of me rescuing Mum then." Pip rubbed her forehead, leaving angry red lines in her skin with her fingers.

"You have decided then? That's my girl. I knew you would."

"But Sergeant Bunn?" Pip protested.

"Don't worry about that. Toothless will really have nothing to lose now. Get yourself dressed. Let's go home."

19

* * *

"Come and sit down. I need to talk to you." Pip was hardly through the door before Toothless gave her stern instruction. She had just scoffed a family-size pork pie. Savoury jelly was smeared around her mouth and shiny pastry flakes wafted a path from her neck to her lap.

"We had that blasted policeman here today." Pip's face reddened. She drew a wobbly chair from under the kitchen table and turned it to face Toothless who, as usual, was basking in the warm glow of the fire from her armchair. Nurse Bladderwash stood with her back to the fire, smoking a cigarette.

"So, Sergeant Bunn is worried about you, Pip," she said, brushing bits of pie onto the floor. "He's concerned about your welfare. He even had the audacity to imply that I might be breaking the law. What have you been saying to him? Hmmm…?"

"Well, I haven't…" Pip began.

"This is how I see it," Toothless raised her voice to cover Pip's. She paused and tried to get up from her armchair. She puffed and gasped as she tried to prise herself up by the armrests. Nothing budged so she gave up; her face turned purple by the wasted effort.

"This is how I see it," she said angrily. "Nothing in life is free, my dear Pip. Everything comes with a price. You've spent too long here free-loading." A wry smile grew at the corners of Pip's mouth.

"Do you think this is funny? Why, I should…"

"No, Toothless, I'm sorry. Please go on."

"Bladderwash and I have been talking and we have come to the conclusion that you've been taking advantage of our kindness."

Bladderwash nodded her assent and took a drag from her dwindling cigarette. The burning tip was perilously close to her thin lips. She picked it away in time and tossed it into the fire.

"In what way?" Pip asked.

"Do I really have to spell it out to you?" Globules of sweat had gathered on Toothless' top lip.

"I'd like it if you did."

20

"Well, the CHEEK!" Toothless bellowed. She shook her head and sent sweat flying into the fire. The flames hissed. She turned her face to Pip.

"The apple really doesn't fall far from the tree, does it? And what a flimsy, rotten old stick of an apple tree your mother was." Pip ground her teeth together at the mention of her mother, making the muscles in her jaw twitch.

"I don't have to stay and listen to this," Pip slapped her hands on the kitchen table and stood up. The chair scraped along the stone floor as she rose to full height. Toothless suddenly burst out laughing.

"Would you look at her?" she wheezed. "The child has spirit, Bladderwash. Maybe she's not so much like her mother after all."

Bladderwash raised a single eyebrow in surprise. Toothless became silent. She thought for a while.

"Sit down, girl. Let's not get overly heated." Pip did as she was told.

"It's time we put you to work." Toothless scratched her chin.

"But I already work for you."

"I mean proper work, girl. Meaningful work. Work that pays for your upkeep. Do you really think what you bring home is a fair exchange for your board and lodgings? It doesn't even cover the coal for our fire."

"YOUR fire, you mean? I can barely feel the heat from it."

"Now listen here, young lady. Your mother left us in the lurch with a young baby. We have cared for you all this time without so much as a penny handout from anyone. It's time you repaid our generosity."

Pip wanted to argue with Toothless, but she knew she had to keep quiet.

"And here's the bonus, young Pip. If you do well on your first outing, we might, just might, be a little bit closer to finding out where your silly mother got to."

"My mum..." Pip got up from her chair again.

"Sit down, Pip; all in good time." Toothless closed her eyes for a few moments, then brought her hands into her lap and interlaced her podgy fingers.

"You might think we've always been digging in the dirt to make our living but no, oh no. Have you never wondered about this grand old house?"

"Well, yes, but…" Toothless ignored her.

"I come from a line of very clever people, don't you know? The very cleverest being Mr John Nash. I'm sure you've heard of him. He was my great-great-great-great-grandfather. The grandfather of the canal if you like. He designed it. And do you know why I closed all the locks and put no entry signs on the towpaths all those years ago?"

Pip shook her head.

"Mr John Nash designed a very clever canal system AND this fabulous house, but apart from that, he added a secret time portal." Toothless looked over at Pip, expecting to see disbelief on her face.

"Oh! Oh, my!" Pip tried to look amazed as if she was hearing the story for the first time.

"Yes, quite unbelievable, isn't it? He had a particular fondness for magic, a fondness that he managed to keep secret, even from his family. We found all sorts of weird and wonderful things in the attic, didn't we, Bladderwash?"

"What sort of things?" Pip asked.

"Oh, charts and wands and masks and potions and skulls. A very strange collection indeed. Most importantly, we found a key-cutting device. Anyway, that's not for you to bother your head with. Your task; Bladderwash and I thought long and hard about this. Eventually, we decided to have a key made for St Petersburg, Russia."

"What?" Pip said.

"Yes, we're starting you off with quite a difficult challenge. You'll find the royal family under house arrest in Alexander Palace. You need to return to 1917. Don't look so gormless, girl. I'll explain how."

"But when?"

"As soon as possible, I'm afraid. Due to Sergeant Bunn's concern over your welfare, we're going to have to get rid of you… I mean, give you a worthwhile job to do as soon as possible. You'll go tonight. I've told him we're sending you away to boarding school."

"Look at her trembling," Nurse Bladderwash said. "There's no use sending a scaredy-cat."

"I'm not scared," Pip said, but she was.

"Good. There's no place for fear in this game. You won't last very long if you're going to let nerves get the better of you. Bladderwash and I had many trips back in time. Didn't we, my friend?"

"Yes," the nurse said, "It was a hoot, and the fun we had when we brought back the spoils."

"Well, enough of that, you'll give the girl ideas." Toothless became serious again.

"Here's how it works. On the far bank of the canal by lock 13, under the weeds right at the bottom, you'll find a grid; a wide iron grid. Attached to the grid is a dial."

Pip was trying to keep a look of shock on her face.

"Don't look so idiotic, child. If you're not up to this, I'm wasting my time telling you about it. We can hand you over to the authorities and that will be the end of it."

"No, Toothless, go on please."

"The dial gives entry to a tunnel that can take you back in time. Turn the dial to the desired year and the grid will slide open. Under the grid, you'll find a hatch with a metal door."

"Slow down," Bladderwash said. "She can't keep up."

"Look, it's not that complicated. The metal door is locked. The tunnel will only work if you have the right key. Bladderwash has been very busy all day with her smelting goggles on. She made you a key for St Petersburg."

"I nearly took my finger off with the key saw," Bladderwash said. Pip noticed the grubby nicotine-stained plaster she'd used to cover the wound.

"Oh, DO stop griping, please. Can you give her the key?"

Bladderwash rummaged around in her pockets and brought out a large, black, wrought-iron key. She dusted bits of tobacco from it with her uninjured hand.

"Come and get it." She held it out for Pip to take. "Thank you, but won't I struggle not being able to understand Russian? Let alone speak it?"

"Ah, she's a bright spark this one. Find her the Russian dictionary Bladderwash; she's got a few hours to swot up. Oh, don't look like that, I'm pulling your leg. When you put the key in the lock, just before you turn it, say these words;

Wheresoever I be going
Make my tongue all language knowing."

Pip repeated the incantation under her breath.

"When you get to the other side, knock three times, easy-peasy. Oh, there's one more thing. Actually, the most important thing of all. The encyclopaedia, Bladderwash."

"Oh yes, one moment."

Bladderwash threw the key at Pip, who caught it with one hand, then reached up to the bookcase.

"'P to R' please; that's the one."

Bladderwash strained under the weight of the book and handed it to Toothless who reached into the pocket of her smock. Where's my special red pen? Ah, here it is. Let me find Russia… da, da, da… Tsar Nicholas… give me a moment, here we are."

Toothless started to make big circles around the pictures in the encyclopaedia with her red pen.

"This, this, this and this. Lovely jewels; we'll have that nice tiara. Ooh, those goblets, and that's a nice brooch. That bracelet looks expensive. Yes, Bladderwash, I think we chose well. We'll be stuffing our pockets with cash after this little haul. Get it, Pip? Your task is to steal all these riches and bring them home to us. Pretend to be a housemaid or something. Use your imagination. Do you think you can do it?"

Pip was now standing between the two women with the key in her hand.

"Yes, yes, I think I can, Toothless. In fact, I know I can."

"Go to bed and have a few hours' sleep then. The portal will only open at midnight. It will let you know when it's time." Pip turned to leave the kitchen

"Oh, and one more thing," Toothless warned. "Don't EVER let any of the people you meet know of their impending doom. Not unless you want to join my four-legged verminous sister in her mouse hole."

"That'll make two of you to chase with my broom," cackled Bladderwash. "Unless she's turned into a dancing Russian bear. She'd be too big to fit back down the tunnel then. What a shame that would be."

"Oh, stop it," Toothless said. She had started to laugh. Her face was red, and she was clutching at her sides. "You'd better start honing your broom skills, my friend," she wheezed.

The laughter followed Pip up the stairs, the cackling and wheezing diminishing with every step she took. She climbed her ladder in silence and flopped onto her bed.

Four

Pip lit a candle and reached into her pocket for Mrs Higgins. The left pocket of her jeans was empty. She tried the right. Frantically, she patted both back pockets. Mrs Higgins wasn't there. She untied her hair and raked her fingers through it, hoping to find her friend snoozing there. Nope, not there either.

She sat down heavily on the bed and looked at her watch. It was seven o'clock. She had five hours before her journey began. She got up again and climbed back down her ladder. She began to step gingerly down the stairs. She needed to find her friend. Having descended one flight, she heard a rustling. She peered down through the banister rails.

Mrs Higgins was struggling up the stairs with a crumpled piece of paper between her teeth. She put it down and looked up at Pip.

"Don't just stand there goggling, give me a hand and quick, they'll be heading for bed soon." Pip was relieved to see her friend.

"What is it? What have you got?"

"I'll tell you in a minute. Quick, help me up."

Pip flew down the stairs and bent to pick up the crumpled piece of paper. She put it in her pocket and held her hand out for her friend to scamper up her arm. She dashed back up the stairs, zipped up the ladder and closed the hatch.

"Where were you?" Pip asked, sitting down on her bed. "I was getting worried." Mrs Higgins had settled on her shoulder.

"I, my dear girl, was preparing for your adventure. Thankfully, Pompeii appears in the same encyclopaedia volume as Russia. I tore the page out while they were gassing. Let me show you. Where is it?"

Pip took the page from her pocket and smoothed it out on her

26

knee. Mrs Higgins had taught her to read using the encyclopaedias. She practically knew every word off by heart.

"I must say," Pip began, "I'd always wondered why they had so much scrawl all over them. I assumed it was a child's scribble."

"You're not too far from the truth. This is the page Toothless showed to your mum before she set off for Pompeii. Let's see what she circled. That way, when you get there, you'll have an idea about where she went to look for the treasure."

"I always loved learning about Pompeii."

"Well, what better way to learn about something than completely immersing yourself in it?"

"I have a job to do," Pip reminded her friend. "Rescuing Mum, remember?"

"That's my girl. Look, most of the items Toothless circled seem to have belonged to the House of the Venus."

"The Venus statuette, the silver wine goblets and the jewellery, yes," Pip agreed.

"You'll find all those things on the Via dell'Abbondanza." Mrs Higgins paused to clean her whiskers.

"She circled a gladiator's shield too. That looks heavy. I wonder if she was caught trying to take it." Pip was thinking about her mum carrying it through the streets of Pompeii without being seen.

"Maybe. That's what you're going to find out. You'll find the gladiators' barracks on the same street. Look at the map there, it's the longest street in Pompeii and the most central."

"A strigil from the Stabian Baths, that's nearby, and that purple brooch came from one of the vineyards, also near to that house," Pip said. A warm feeling of excitement had spread through her body. "Our house was owned by a branch of the Satri family, apparently. I wonder what they were like. I wonder if they captured Mum and were being mean to her."

"What they ARE like, Pip. You'll meet them very soon and they'll be living and breathing as we are now."

"That's a crazy thought."

"Do you think you've got it? Repeat it all back to me."

"I need to find the House of Venus on Via Dell'Abbondanza."

"Good, and what was your mum looking for?"

"Their Venus statuette, their silver goblets with the embossed hunting scenes. Oh, and the amber earrings with matching bracelet."

"Good, what else?"

"The strigil from the Stabian Baths and the gladiator's shield embossed with the gladiator helmet."

"Excellent, but you're missing one item."

"Yes, I was just getting to the purple brooch from the local vineyard."

"Good. What time is it?"

"Seven-thirty," Pip said. "Should I go down and wrestle the key to Pompeii from Toothless now?"

"That's the silliest thing I've ever heard. You need to get some rest. I'll wake you up when they're both fast asleep. Oh, and one more thing. I found a jute potato sack in the barn. I nibbled holes in it for your head and arms."

"You did what?"

"Do you expect to waltz around Pompeii in your jeans and anorak? Hm…?"

"I hadn't thought of that. Mrs Higgins, you're the best."

"Well, I've used the tunnel before, don't forget. The potato sack will pass for a Roman tunic. I even managed to stitch a pocket in for you. Tie it at the waist with a length of baling twine, also at the back door. I think it's best if you try to pass yourself off as a boy. Girls didn't have the freedom to roam, so they'll think you're a boy anyway, most likely. Life was dangerous for girls in ancient Rome."

"Thank you," Pip said. "I wish you were coming with me."

"You don't need me anymore, Pip, you'll see. Get some sleep now; I'll give your ear a nibble when it's time."

Pip sat up and rubbed her eyes.

"That was quite a hard nip."

"Was it? Sorry, I'm a bit nervous."

"If you're nervous, how do you think I'm feeling?"

"Nervous in a good way," the mouse said clapping her tiny paws together. "Nervously excited."

"What time is it?"

"The kitchen clock said eleven."

"Not long to go then." Pip swung her legs over the side of the bed. "I'm not sure I can do it, not on my own."

"I have faith in you, Pip and so does your mum. She's waiting for you to come and rescue her."

"But what if I get lost like her? Or worse? What if…?"

"If I didn't think you were up to it, I wouldn't let you go. You can do it." Mrs Higgins interrupted. "Come on. Get yourself dressed."

Pip did as she was told then asked, "What else do I need?"

"Just yourself, oh, and bring the matches," the mouse said before jumping into Pip's hair.

Pip wanted to jump on the banister, fly down and run away, but she thought of her mum alone in Pompeii and steeled herself. She began the descent gingerly in the dark, not wanting to encourage the tiniest of creaks from the old stairs. The more steps she tiptoed down, the louder Toothless' snores became and the brighter became the light from a half-moon that peered through the landing windows.

At last, she reached the ground floor. Mrs Higgins swung down on a strand of hair to whisper in her ear;

"Open her bedroom door but do it gently; the knob needs oiling. When you're inside, strike a match and I'll get to work."

"What do you mean?" Pip said. "Don't I have to grab the key from around her neck?"

"That'll wake her up instantly. The one good thing about being a mouse, my girl, is the teeth." She snapped them together for effect. Pip laughed. "Shoosh! You'll wake old Bladderwash. Go on, try the door."

Pip grasped the old brass doorknob. It was cold to the touch. She turned it slowly. There was a short creak as it gave way. She pushed the door gently and slid through the crack. She left it ajar for a quick escape. Toothless continued to snore.

Once inside, she reached into her pocket for the matches. She struck one and held her breath. She'd never been inside Toothless' bedroom before. It was a mass of clutter and junk. She could barely make out the bed in all the rubbish, but she noticed the rise and fall of Toothless' body. It moved in time with her snores.

She crept over to the bed and kicked over a glass that had been left on the floor. She held her breath as it knocked the floorboard then spun around. It came to a halt and Pip exhaled. Toothless continued to snore. She stood back as Mrs Higgins darted over the newspapers and bits of discarded food on the bedspread. The mouse found the flesh around Toothless' neck and scrabbled around for the cord that held the key.

The match in Pip's fingers spluttered then went out. She quickly lit another.

Seconds later, Mrs Higgins had the dirty twine in her teeth and began to gnaw furiously.

"Done it," she hissed at Pip. "Come and get the key."

Pip edged over. With one hand, she leant on the bed. She held the match in her teeth. Her other hand reached over the mound that was Toothless. She pulled gently at the severed string until the big black key appeared at the neck of the woman's nightgown. As soon as she saw it, she wrapped her fingers around it and drew it away.

"That's it. You've got it," Mrs Higgins said.

Suddenly, Toothless' hand rose from the bed and she slapped herself around the jowls. "Stop it! You're tickling me," she said playfully. She grunted and made a choking noise. Coming to her senses, she sat up. Mrs Higgins darted from the bedspread. Pip quickly blew out the match but it was too late.

"What on EARTH are you doing in my room, you vile creature?" She felt around her neck for the key to Pompeii. "THE KEY! THE KEY! Bladderwash, where are you?"

Pip was considering staying to make up an excuse, but sense told her to run. She stuffed the key into her pocket and slipped out of the bedroom door. She knew it would take Toothless a while to haul herself out of bed.

She rushed into the kitchen to be met by a slender figure standing by the empty hearth. The orange glow from a cigarette lit the form of Mrs Higgins, being dangled dangerously by her tail by a spindly finger and thumb.

"Is this what you're looking for?" Bladderwash asked, swinging the mouse in small circles.

"Mrs Higgins!" Pip cried.

"She told you about Pompeii, didn't she? She helped you take the key. Well, my girl, you've been well and truly caught now, haven't you?"

"Run, Pip," squeaked the mouse. "Run to the canal. Do it. Don't worry about me."

Toothless appeared at the door, panting.

"Why, that ungrateful little wretch. Grab her, Bladderwash, in fact, I'll grab her myself." She lunged forwards, one hand on her nightgown, the other making its way towards Pip's throat.

"Come and get me then," Pip goaded. She danced toward Toothless, then away again until Toothless made a final lunge with all her weight behind it. Pip darted out of the way in time and Toothless went crashing into Bladderwash, both of them falling to the ground. Toothless pinned the smaller woman under her great weight and lay on top of her, unable to get herself up again. Her arms flailed around helplessly, every movement crushing her friend further into the stone floor.

Pip bent down and teased Bladderwash's gnarled fingers away from her friend. She flung the mouse roughly into her hair and galloped towards the back door.

"See you soon," she shouted. "I'm going to rescue my mum."

"You'll do no such thing," Toothless puffed, her face a deep shade of purple. "You'll be back here begging for forgiveness in no time, or better still, squeaking for forgiveness."

"Or grunting, or baaing," wheezed Bladderwash.

Pip left the women rolling around on the floor and slammed the back door. She quickly gathered up her Roman outfit and raced out of the yard. She fixed the padlock to the iron gate, locked it and took the key with her, just in case Toothless managed to get herself to her feet and follow her.

31

"Nicely done, Pip," said Mrs Higgins, emerging from Pip's hair to sit on her shoulder. "You'd better get a move on though, the kitchen clock said ten to midnight."

Pip hurried along the dark canal bank. The moon had been covered by cloud and it had started to rain. She pulled up the hood on her anorak as she passed through the first tunnel on her way to the thirteenth lock. A few pigeons buffeted against each other on the ridge overhead, cooing quietly. She could see their red feet and broken claws clinging to the ledge.

As she emerged from the tunnel, the rain fell more heavily. She shivered and thrust her hands into her pockets.

"I'm going to miss you, Pip," Mrs Higgins said from the comfort of her hood.

"I don't want to go alone."

"You'll be fine, I promise. You don't want an old rodent tagging along, cramping your style."

"Oh, but I do, Mrs Higgins, I really do."

Pip pressed on to her usual swimming spot. She'd never been this far after dark before, but she knew the canal well and the absence of light didn't matter too much.

"You'd better hurry and get changed," the mouse piped up, "before Toothless raises the alarm." She scampered out of the hood, down Pip's legs and onto the ground.

Pip hid behind the bush and put on her new tunic.

"It's itchy," she complained, and I'm FREEZING cold."

"You'll be much colder in the canal."

"Yes, that's very helpful, thanks," Pip said, hiding her clothes deep within the bushes, "They're going to get wet," she moaned as rain fell into her face.

"That's the least of your worries now. Come on, get yourself in and off."

She hunched up her shoulders against the cold and squatted down on the canal bank. She slowly lowered herself in.

"Brr…," her teeth chattered as she drew her face level with her friend's.

"Watch out for the broom," she said to the mouse. "I expect you to be alive and well when I return with Mum."

"You can count on that," her friend replied, tears gathering in the corners of her tiny eyes.

"Thank you, Mrs Higgins," Pip said, holding out her finger. The mouse grabbed it and shook it vigorously. Pip picked up the big iron key with her free hand and placed it between her teeth.

"Best of British," squeaked the mouse. "See you soon." She let go of Pip's finger and watched proudly as she flipped around to dive under the water.

Pip swam to the far side of the canal and nearing Lock Thirteen, came up for breath. Her face was met by pelting rain. She reached up for the white wooden arm to hold herself steady while she surveyed the bank. The coots seemed to be in their nests. She dropped back into the water.

She began to methodically run her hands over the canal bed, feeling for the iron grid Toothless and Mrs Higgins had told her about. She felt slimy stones and plenty of silt and muck but nothing hard and metallic. She felt something cold move against her leg and froze. It was a big old fish swimming a figure of eight through her legs.

She started to panic, coming up again for air. She was sure it was close to midnight. She saw a flash of lightning cut through the downpour. It bounced over the water and she saw a glint of something catch its light a short distance from her feet. She quickly dived towards the shimmer.

Suddenly, the whole bed of the canal was covered by blue light. "The canal will let you know when it's midnight," Pip remembered Toothless' words. The light came from a dense patch of weeds. She parted them to reveal the grid she had been looking for. She passed her hands over it, desperately searching for a dial.

The grid was round and made of latticed metal. She felt around its rim until her hands came upon a metal chain. She took hold of it and gave it a sharp tug. A clap of thunder made her jump as a clod of earth freed itself from the canal bed. Desperately, she pulled away all the muck that had collected on the dial since her mother had taken hold of it thirteen long years ago.

Pip held the dial into the blue light and peered at it. It was fashioned like a combination lock similar to an old-fashioned bicycle lock. She had found plenty of those discarded in the canal and knew how to open them. She spun the number around until the dial read 0079, the year she needed for Pompeii. She heard a creak, then an eerie scraping as the grid started to move. It slid away from her, revealing a hard black metal door.

She felt with her fingers for a keyhole, then took the key from between her teeth. She thrust it into the lock.

'Wheresoever I be going
Make my tongue all language knowing.'

Her words were muffled by the thick canal water; she felt a sharp pain then an electric tingle in her tongue. She turned the key and the door flew open, knocking her sideways. The water around her started to churn. It tossed her around until she was upside down, then with one great gulp, she was sucked through the door headfirst.

Pip had been drawn into a narrow water-filled pipe. She was being pulled so hard that she was spiralling downwards, clanking and crashing against the sides. She could see nothing in the pitch black.

With a sudden and painful thud, her head hit the bottom. She ignored the impulse to breathe in. She had been holding her breath for a long time now and was starting to feel dizzy. Gathering all the strength she had left, she squeezed herself up tightly to try and turn around. She almost had to fold herself in two, the pipe was so tight. Eventually, she righted herself. She bent her knees and gave an almighty push through her feet.

Up and up she sailed, and, as she did, the darkness started to clear. Then, as suddenly as her head had hit the bottom, it thumped against the top. She knocked three times and waited. She waited and waited. She could feel her face getting fat and red. She put one hand over her mouth and pinched her nose with the other to stop herself from breathing in.

At last, she heard the familiar creaking of the moving grid. Slowly, it slid over her head. She looked up and had to squint her eyes against a dazzling light. She swam out of the tunnel and towards the light as fast as her legs could propel her and heard the grid grinding as it closed behind her.

Five

As Pip's head broke the surface of the beautifully clear water, she took gulps of clean, delicious air.

She looked up into a cloudless sky and sighed. She had found herself in a small clear pool by a clutch of olive trees. She swam to the edge, a bright sun already warming her skin. She got out of the pool and curled up under one of the trees.

Pip slept soundly until the muted clanking of cattle bells woke her up. There was dew on the grass and the morning sun was low in the east. She must have slept all night. She was startled and didn't know where she was for a moment. Then she felt the warm sun on her face and the memory of her time-tunnel journey zipped through her mind. She sat up and rubbed her eyes.

"Hey kid," the man standing by the cattle cart said to her, "come here a minute and hold this beast while I sort myself out. She'll trample the vines otherwise and I'll be in trouble with the boss again."

Pip sprang up and hurried to the man who was hopping awkwardly from one leg to the other. He was wearing an outfit similar to hers. He thrust a thick leather rein into her hand and darted behind an olive tree to relieve himself.

Pip cast her eyes upon the animal at the other end of the rein. The white cow was huge with an enormous lump on her neck where the yoke rested. A meaty blue tongue lolled from her mouth, covered in drool. The cow smelt hot and musty, a bit like a wet dog. Pip stroked her between the ears. The cow swished her tail.

When the man had finished his business, he reappeared from behind the tree, thanked Pip for helping him, and handed her two juicy peaches from the hundreds piled up in his cart. He clicked his tongue to drive the cart onwards.

"Don't lie about in the sun all day, boy, you'll get burned," he advised over his shoulder, "and everyone knows if you sleep under an olive tree, its roots will grow through your ears and into your brain."

Pip laughed. "Thanks for the peaches," she shouted as they left. The cart creaked and shuddered over the uneven path until it became a tiny speck in the distance.

Washing the peaches in the pool, she thought about the man mistaking her for a boy. She hadn't had to try much. Her outfit alone had done the trick. She devoured the peaches greedily, sucking every last bit of sweet stringy flesh from the stones.

Pip then decided to climb one of the olive trees to see where she was in relation to the town. She scratched her knees on the gnarled and twisted old wood as she scaled its branches. Everywhere she looked, a brilliant green was reflected by the sun. A mountain loomed from afar. 'Vesuvius,' she mused.

Even Vesuvius was lined with vines and fruit trees. The volcano looked sleepy. Every so often, a small puff of smoke chuffed from its top, innocent like a sleeping dragon.

Pip turned her head in the other direction. She saw the town encircled by a wall and a beautiful turquoise sea just beyond it. Between her clump of olive trees and the town were several farm buildings, vineyards and fields of sheep. Knowing she had to find the house on the Via dell'Abbondanza, she decided to follow the path the cartman took. He was probably heading to town to sell his peaches.

She jumped from her tree and began her journey. The soft stony earth didn't hurt her feet even though she wasn't wearing shoes. The warm sun beat upon her face and made her smile. She reached a vineyard and hopped over a small gulley separating it from the path. She couldn't resist twisting a large bunch of purple grapes from the vine.

It shone with a silver bloom. She crouched down in the gully to eat the grapes, savouring every one. Each fruit burst in her mouth, the bitterness of the skin mingling with the sweetness of the flesh.

Satisfied, and licking purple juice from her chin, she jumped up, wiping her hands on her tunic.

"Not so fast, sonny Jim." Pip felt a large pair of hands clamp roughly on her shoulders. She twisted around, trying to free herself.

"Let me go!" She reached behind and tried to prise away the fingers clamped to her.

"I suppose you thought you could help yourself to my prize crop, did you? A free breakfast, was it?" Pip managed to turn around, but the man's hands still held her fast. She looked up into his face. His lips were thin and cruel, and spittle had formed at the corners of his mouth. His anger had forced a dewdrop of snot out of his head. It wobbled precariously from his left nostril.

"Well, speak up, boy! Who do you belong to? I'll be having a few words with whoever it is. I swear on almighty Bacchus, as true as my name is Octavius Bibulus, I'll have you flogged at dawn and thrown in the bear pit. I swear to Bacchus I'll…"

Pip didn't wait for Octavius to finish his tirade. She gave him a sharp kick in the shins which made him hop madly and let go of her.

"Why, I'll…" he threatened after her, but Pip sped off as fast as she could.

At a safe distance from the angry farmer, she slowed down and caught her breath. She carried on her journey towards the town, nervous now and shaken.

As the path sloped downwards, a large farmhouse came into view. Its walls were painted white and the sun's rays made the tiles on its roof gleam. As she walked closer, she heard voices. Worried about being seen again, she ducked down behind a bush.

In the field to the right of the path, a group of women were laughing and singing as they picked fruit from trees. Too engrossed with their work, Pip was able to nip out from behind the bush and hurry away.

The path led on to the back of the farmhouse where a man was rolling a very large clay jar along its courtyard. The man looked up. He had seen her.

"Hey, boy!" he called over. "There's no time for idling. I have twelve of these olive oil jars to bury before sundown. Who do you belong to? I'll lend your master my mule if you come and give a hand." Pip ran away again. She couldn't risk being caught at this stage in the game. She wasn't safe here. That had been made perfectly clear.

She ran until she knew she was out of sight of the farm. As the town drew nearer, the path became wider and harder under her feet. The rough earth turned gradually to cobbles. The green fields and fruit trees had been left behind.

Larger, more imposing trees now lined what had become a substantial road. Every now and then, she passed a stone tomb or a more elaborate mausoleum. She stopped to touch a marble statue at the entrance to a very grand monument. It felt cool in spite of the warm sun. She noticed a small bowl at the feet of the statue. In it were figs and walnuts. They looked very tasty, but Pip knew better than to steal from the dead.

She was thankful for her good manners, as, without warning, a large family appeared at the next tomb along. She hurried by with her head down.

She had almost reached the town walls. Traffic was getting heavier. More people began to appear on the pavements. Some were laughing and joking, some lost in thought. She saw a mother scold her child as he stepped out in front of a donkey carrying a load of heavy stones.

Nobody seemed interested in Pip and she was glad after her tussle with Octavius. She crossed the road and ran her hands along the stone city wall. It felt cold and rough under her fingers. At the end of the wall was the city entrance. She passed the gates, glancing in at the buildings and cobbled streets, deciding to walk to the harbour before she entered.

She passed a temple on her way to the water. A small group of men had gathered around a statue at the entrance. One of the men was kneeling at the statue's feet while the others were goading him;

"Hurry up, Felix, we'll miss today's catch. It's already late. You've practically rubbed her feet away with your hot little hands."

"We're late because you stayed up all night praying to Bacchus with your face in a wine goblet," Felix said, "and you'll be sorry when we're tossed into the briny because we didn't ask Venus to watch over us."

Felix reluctantly stood up and the other men clapped him on the back and jeered. "You'd be better off praying to Isis for safe return. What's the deal with Venus anyway? Are you hoping she'll make your wife more beautiful?"

The fishermen jostled each other down the temple steps, laughing and still jeering at their friend. Pip followed them to the harbour. Small wooden boats bobbed in the water that lapped against the harbour walls. She watched as another group of fishermen returned with a boat full of fish. Noticing the men Pip had seen at the temple, one shouted over to them;

"Sorry, lads, we've got the lot. You're too late." The other men in the boat whooped and hooted, picking up baskets laden with fish to show their competitors. Felix was slapped around the head by his friends;

"That's your fault," they shouted at him.

Turning from the harbour, Pip walked a while and found a sandy cove. She made her way to the water's edge and sat down. She let the water lap over her toes. It felt good. The rhythm of the tide concentrated her mind. She thought about her mum.

Would they recognise each other? Pip had only seen her mum in an old crumpled photograph, and she had been a baby when her mum had seen her last. What if her mum didn't return because she had found happiness in Pompeii? What if she never found her, or worse, what if her mother was dead?

There was no point being negative, she thought to herself and she started to make a plan. Today she would find the House of Venus and work out a way of getting inside. Maybe seeing the Temple of Venus was a good omen. She hoped it was.

Jumping up, she brushed sand from her tunic. Habit made her pat her pocket to feel for Mrs Higgins. Remembering she was alone, she sighed. She missed her friend.

She made her way back towards the town, and, reaching the Temple of Venus, she climbed the steps leading to her statue. She rubbed the goddess's feet as Felix had done and asked for her help in finding her mother. It was worth a try, she thought optimistically. She left the temple and entered Pompeii through the sea gate.

Pip stopped and gazed around;

"Get out of the way, idiot boy," yelled a man from atop a mule. It caught her shoulder and sent her spinning into the gutter as it trotted past. She realised she'd been standing in the middle of the road. She climbed up onto a steppingstone and hopped to the pavement on the other side of the road.

She caught a whiff of something unpleasant, and looking down, at her tunic, saw a large brown watery stain creeping across it. She looked back to where she had fallen. A large pile of dung steamed in the gutter.

Noticing a water fountain not so far away, she made her way a little further up the pavement and joined a long queue of sleepy women who were filling water jugs. When it was her turn, she rinsed herself off.

"Look at the slave boy giving himself a wash and brush up," one of the women behind her said. "Thinks he's a right gentleman. He must think water grows on trees, wasting it like that…" Pip was embarrassed. With a red face, she moved on.

The road became busier as it moved deeper into town. Carts carrying sacks of grain heralded their arrival with tinkling bells. Donkeys carrying baskets full of loaves on their backs tried to squeeze by. Buildings sprang up on both sides of the road, some low, some two or even three storeys high.

Pip looked into one of the shop fronts that opened out onto the street. Just inside the shop, a man was slotting a jar overflowing with olives into the counter;

"What do you want, kid?" he asked. "Here, take these but don't tell the boss." The man handed Pip the olives that had spilled from the jar. They were rich and black, salty and fleshy. She gobbled them instantly, spitting the stones into her hand. "Boy, you must be starving. You'd better take this too." He handed her a large chunk of bread from behind the counter.

"Thank you," she called after the man who had already left the shop to fetch more jars.

Pip threw the olive stones into the gutter and demolished the bread in seconds.

She could see the looming forum straight ahead of her and remembered that it led onto the Via dell'Abbondanza. She crossed the road again once it was free of traffic. She used the steppingstones this time to keep her feet out of the dung, vegetable peelings and bits of broken crockery that had gathered there in a jumble.

Leaving the vast columns of the forum behind, she took her first steps onto the Via dell'Abbondanza, the road that would hopefully lead her to her mother. Small posts had been built at the entrance to keep carts out. It was wide and lined with trees. The road here was smooth, not rutted by wagon wheels like the roads by the shops. There was a group of men huddled beneath a wide arch. They were talking loudly, blocking the entrance to other men who wanted to go inside;

"No point coming any further," one of the men advised the hopeful bathers. "The Stabian Baths are as dry as a bone. Try the forum baths."

Pip crossed the road and walked on. The further she walked, the grander the houses became. She remembered the map Mrs Higgins had shown her. She should find the House of Venus on the south side of the street quite near the far end. Suddenly, out of nowhere, two boys carrying writing tablets ran into her, knocking her down for the second time that day. Neither looked back to see that she was alright. They were red-faced and panting;

"I'm not being whipped again," the one in front shouted. "I'd rather do a month of algebra than be whipped again for lateness."

"Wait for me," the other wheezed. "I have a stone in my sandal."

The boy stopped and shook the stone from his shoe before dashing on to his lessons at the forum.

Pip picked herself up and continued her search for the house. The road was long, and she passed several grand houses. Voices interrupted Pip's train of thought. She looked up and saw two men standing talking in a doorway. She recognised the taller man and a tingle of fear crept through her. It was Octavius, the angry farmer whose grapes she had eaten.

Quickly, she crossed the road and hid behind a tree. Peering around it, she could just about hear the conversation;

"I don't know why you don't just let your slaves get on with it, Stephanus. Why do you have to meddle with it? How difficult can it be to run a laundry these days?"

"Come now, Octavius," Stephanus said, shielding his eyes from the sun. "I need things done JUST right and if I'm not there to oversee things, well, you never know what might happen."

"For the love of Bacchus, man, all they do is slosh around in urine all day long. What could possibly go wrong?"

"You'd be surprised," Stephanus replied. He had a small rasping voice. Pip had to strain to hear him.

"Suit yourself," Octavius said, "but I trust you'll be attending the baths sometime this week? You need to keep up with things. We need to speak to Gaius about this dratted situation with the water. Have you seen the queues at the fountains? Damned ridiculous."

"Yes, of course. It's affecting my business too. I'll see you very soon, Octavius. Give my love to Valentina." Stephanus crept back into the doorway and Octavius swished away in his purple robes, heading into town.

Pip emerged from behind her tree and pressed on, staying on the north side of the road. She was nearing the end of the street now, so she was close to the House of Venus. Several large houses stood on the opposite side of the road. How would she know which one was hers?

She didn't have to wonder for long. Two children burst out of one of the houses, a boy of about ten and a younger girl;

"Give him to me, Lucius; give him to me or I'll tell Marcus." The small girl jumped up at her brother who was holding something in his hands, high out of her reach.

"Nope, shan't," Lucius taunted her. "In fact, I'm going to put him on Venus' head, ha, ha…"

43

"You can't do that. He'll fall off and die, and anyway, Mummy has told us we're not allowed to go next door because Mr Satri gets cross."

"Lucius, Tiberia, come here NOW!" a deep bellow stopped the children's argument.

"You've done it now, Tiberia; now we're both in trouble. Marcus has seen you."

A very large man walked over to the children and spoke;

"What are you doing over here in the Satri's garden? If you damage that statue again, you'll be in REAL trouble. Get back inside. Now!"

"Lucius stole my dormouse and he said he was going to put him on Venus' head and…"

"Nobody likes a tell-tale, Tiberia," Marcus said smiling. He put his arm gently around the girl and guided her back into the house.

"Lucius, give her the mouse back; don't be an idiot."

Pip now knew where the House of Venus was. It looked quiet. The shutters were closed and the garden was empty. Was her mum inside? The thought made her shiver. She decided to return to her clump of olive trees and spend the night hatching a plan.

She hurried to the end of the street and left Pompeii by the Sarno Gate. The road from this gate joined up with the one that had taken her into town, and she made her way back to her cluster of olive trees by the pool.

She spent some time in the late afternoon sun, lying on a patch of grass hidden from the path by shrubs. She bathed in the pool. How different it was to the grubby old canal. When she looked down as she trod water, she could see her feet, the water was so clean. When she felt sleepy, she gathered some soft bracken to make a nest behind the shrubs.

She lay on her back and thought hard. She wasn't able to think for long though, as images of Venus swirled in her head. She stretched and yawned. A snapping twig pulled her out of a half-sleep. She sat up and looked around in the gloom. 'Probably a fox', she thought to herself, settling down again. She couldn't see Octavius peering over the shrubs at her in the dark.

Six

Pip woke with a start. Looking up from her pillow of moss and twigs, she felt the early morning sun pushing its way over the grass and soil to heat the earth and light the coming day.

She rose, walked to the pool and bent down to wash her face in the cool water.

She knew it was early. The birds in the trees were still singing out their dawn chorus. This was good. It would give her time to spy on the House of Venus when it was still quiet.

She set off for town. Vesuvius was dozing under a crumpled eiderdown of mist. It chuffed out the occasional cloud of grey smoke. Pip joined the uneven path, moist with morning dew and picked her way through the soil and stones until she reached the vineyards.

Suddenly, a figure moved in the distance. Octavius was running full pelt towards her;

"Stop, thief!" he shouted. "Stop at once. I've reported you to the night-watchmen. I've seen you sleeping in the olive grove. You're a runaway slave and need to be locked in chains. Stop at once, I say!"

Pip quickly twisted a bunch of grapes from the vines and sped away. She ran as fast as she could. She ran all the way to the Stabian Gate. Lucky for her, Octavius had run out of steam and returned to his house. She took a moment to catch her breath, crouching against the city walls, then she ate her breakfast. She was hungry.

Pip was disturbed by voices and the clattering of metal on metal. She tried to make herself small against the wall. Two men were leaving the town. They carried buckets. One had an axe. They were the town's night-watchmen heading back to their barracks.

Pip held her breath. One of the men sensed her presence and turned around.

"What are you doing there, boy? Whose slave are you?" The man put down his buckets and grabbed her roughly by the tunic. He hauled her onto her feet. Pip thought quickly.

"I belong to Mr Octavius, sir," she said, trying to step away from his grasp.

"Well, that's funny because we had a report from the very same Mr Octavius last night about a runaway slave boy sleeping in the hills. He said he would have nabbed the devil himself but was afraid of being kicked again. Nasty little brute, he said."

"Yes, I know," Pip said, "I've been on the lookout for him too. A rough sort, apparently; he's been helping himself to my master's grapes."

"Does Mr Octavius know you're creeping around the town walls in the half-light?" the other man asked.

"He sent me to the town with a message," Pip said. "I tripped and fell here. I'll be on my way now." She twisted free and made to leave.

"Not so fast matey-boy. How do we know you're not the runaway slave? Or worse, a burglar? There's been a spate of burglaries around here recently. Only last week we caught someone trying to pilfer stuff from the House of Venus. Little did she know she'd have US to contend with."

"Oh," said Pip, "A woman? What did you do with her?"

"Never mind that!" The man carrying the axe was becoming impatient. "Who is your message for?"

"Um…" Pip remembered the conversation she overheard yesterday, "It's for Stephanus the fuller. I'm to tell him about a business meeting at the Forum Baths because the Stabian Baths have run dry. The meeting is tomorrow. He needs to know urgently."

"Sounds legit," said the man with the axe, turning to his friend.

"Hm, I dunno," said the other, "maybe we should walk him to the door."

"You do what you want. You spent most of the night snoring. Don't think I didn't see you curled up on the forum steps. I spent the night

46

patrolling the city. I'm tired and want my bed." The man with the axe turned and headed away from the town.

"Off you go then, sonny," the other man said, cuffing Pip around the head. "No more loitering." He picked up his buckets and strode off.

Pip didn't hang around to watch the two men head home to their barracks. She ducked through the gates and made her way to the Via dell'Abbondanza. It MUST have been her mum the night-watchmen were talking about. She'd been caught then. Would she still be in the house? She doubted it.

Pip made her way to the House of Venus and crossed the road to hide behind a tree. People were starting to emerge in the street. Shutters were flung open and slaves were leaving houses to run errands. She saw the big man she'd seen with the children the day before leaving his house. He had a scroll under his arm and strode away towards the forum.

She peered from around the tree at the House of Venus. The shutters were still closed. If only she could get inside, just to ask someone what had happened to her mum. She waited and waited.

Eventually, the shutters broke. A slave girl leaned from the window and looked up and down the street. Pip heard some shouting and the girl disappeared again. After what seemed like an eternity, the front door opened, and an older woman stepped out.

She was dressed in a dark green stola. She looked elegant as she walked through the front garden onto the pavement.

Pip assumed the woman was Mrs Satri. The slave girl Pip had seen in the window dashed out after her. She heard her being scolded. They started to walk towards the forum. Pip decided to follow them. She waited a few moments then set off on the other side of the street.

She passed the Stabian Baths which now had a barricade across the entrance. The road was getting busier. A number of people had appeared; all heading for the forum. Mrs Satri and the girl had now crossed to her side of the street. Pip picked up her speed, not wanting to lose sight of her.

They left the Via dell'Abbondanza and entered the square that led to the forum buildings. It was market day. People were beginning to mill around various stores and barrows selling what, she couldn't quite see.

It wasn't long before Mrs Satri, the slave girl and Pip herself became part of the throng. She made sure to keep them both in her sight.

Mrs Satri stopped at a fabric stall. She touched a length of crimson material being shown to her by a salesman. He unrolled it, urging her to make a purchase. Pip decided to approach her now and ask her what had happened to her mum.

She nudged her way closer. "Excuse me," she pleaded desperately to the people blocking her view of Mrs Satri who was now walking away from the cloth stall. Panic gripped her. She didn't have long to rescue her mum. "Excuse me, please," she repeated as she bumped her way through a sea of people, trying not to lose sight of her.

Pip managed to keep Mrs Satri in her vision as she passed vegetable stalls, stalls with tall piles of crockery and religious statuettes. She passed men selling sausages and tiny pots of roasted chickpeas. She hurried after her until Mrs Satri stopped in a clearing. Pip stopped too.

In the middle of the clearing, Pamphilus the slave trader, a small stocky man, was standing on a box. He held a long whip that he cracked every now and then to the delight of the crowd that had gathered around him. Pip forgot about Mrs Satri for the moment. The man had the audience captivated.

"Thank you, sir, a fabulous sale. You won't be sorry. Now, can you bring the next one in? Yes, of course I'm ready," Pamphilus directed Agrippa, his assistant.

"Ladies and gentlemen, good fellows of Pompeii. Who will give me two thousand for this very fine specimen?"

A young man was brought into the ring, paraded around for a few circuits, then forced to stand on a revolving plinth. Nausea crept over Pip. This was a slave auction.

"Who will give me two thousand for him?" Pamphilus went on, "I guarantee you won't get a better price anywhere else."

Pip stared at the man standing on the plinth. One of his feet had been painted white and a wooded plaque hung around his neck, stating his origin; he was from Spain. He looked afraid as some members of the audience gathered around him.

"Now then, sonny, don't be shy. Puff out that chest, that's it," the slave-seller goaded. He turned to the crowd; "Come and inspect this fine hunk of flesh! That's it, madam, come and have a feel. Good, eh? Fancy him, do you?"

Pip felt sick and turned away. She remembered Mrs Satri who had wandered away. She was talking to some people on the other side of the clearing. She pushed her way through the crowd. As she drew closer, she saw that Mrs Satri was talking to Octavius. She also recognised the very big man she'd seen with the children. He still had the scroll under his arm. She got near enough to hear their conversation. Octavius was in full command of everyone's attention;

"I dare say, I'll bid for her myself."

"Who?" Marcus, the big man asked.

"The rotten cur they caught in the Satri household, of course; the unwashed harpy. She had my purple brooch. The absolute impertinence of it. She'd obviously been on a spree, helping herself to everyone's treasured possessions. The watchmen caught her the other night. She put up a ferocious fight apparently, which is what gave me my terrific idea. Lucky for her, and me, the authorities sold her to Pamphilus."

"Oh darling, we don't need another slave. You have too many already; quite a collection," Valentina, Octavius' wife said.

"Nonsense, my dear, one can never have enough slaves, and anyway, I have special plans for this one."

"Oh?" said Marcus, "Maybe Mrs Satri should have the first bid, considering she was caught in her house."

"Oh no, thank you very much," said Mrs Satri. "I have my slave girl here to look after and I certainly don't want a thief in the household to keep my eyes on." She turned to Marcus, "What are you doing here?"

"A little business for Mr Gaius; we've just made the purchase of a slave boy. We liked the look of the Greek lad. The plan is to train him up to replace me when I get my freedom. They're holding onto him until Gaius gets back from the temple."

"Oh, very good," Mrs Satri said. "Shouldn't be long now until you're freed, though I don't know how Gaius will cope without you."

"Just another ten years, Mrs Satri," said Marcus, smiling.

"Hush now," Octavius said. "The house-breaking vixen should be up next."

Pip pushed back through the crowd in a frenzy. She wriggled through the rabble until she was right at the front. The slave-seller was finishing business from his last sale.

"That's right, sir, gladiator material; maybe next year's games if you treat him well," he paused, "Or badly!" He stopped his delivery to roar at his joke, contained himself then went on, "All done then? Sold to the slave of Alianus Favonius. Can you take him round the back for the formalities please, Agrippa? Thank you."

Pip watched as the slave was led away like an animal. Nobody in the crowd seemed moved by his treatment. They stood around, muttering idly.

"Now, what have we next?" the slave-trader was about to introduce his next sale. "Ah yes, an interesting lot this one. Agrippa," he called to his assistant, "the cat burglar please, thank you."

Pip stared at the plinth her mum was being led to. All her blood rushed to her head which pounded with every beat of her heart. "Mum," she whispered at first, then she said it more loudly, then she shouted, "Mum! Mum!"

Her shouts were drowned out by Octavius who had elbowed his way to the front of the crowd.

"I'll have that one if you don't mind," he roared at the slave-seller.

"Oh, I DO like an easy sale," Pamphilus said, turning to Octavius, "Don't know much about this one. She wouldn't say where she comes from. She's got spirit though; I'll tell you that for nothing. Best for the fields, maybe, just don't leave her with your best silver, ha, ha…"

"I'll give you fifteen hundred," Octavius interrupted him. "Have her sent to the farm." With that, he turned and made his way back through the crowd.

Pip watched helplessly as her mum was led away. She decided to creep around to the back of the tent where the slaves were being held to rescue her. She'd fight if she had to. She had no choice.

All of a sudden, Pip felt a low and very deep rumble pass beneath her feet. The crowd stopped muttering. Pamphilus stopped shouting. Another louder rumble came up through the ground. A woman in the audience let out a yelp. A third rumble, bolstered by a sharp splitting noise, sent Pamphilus crashing from his stool onto the floor.

The ground was now shaking. Pip did all she could to stay on her feet. Was this the eruption? Was Vesuvius about to blow its top?

Deafening screams rose from the crowd;

"May the Gods save us!" someone shouted as he clutched his wife in panic.

"We have angered the Gods!" screamed another. "Bacchus, keeper of Pompeii, protect us from mighty Jupiter!" he yelled to no avail.

"For the Gods' sakes, I've only just mended my roof after the last earthquake," complained a more practically minded man in the crowd.

Pip looked around her as the floor continued to shake. Stalls had been upturned and pottery smashed. Vegetables were rolling around on the ground having fallen from displays. The people who had been left on their feet started to fall over the rolling vegetables.

In the commotion, Pip noticed Agrippa trying to hold onto the slave Pamphilus had sold first. He wriggled free and escaped through the stumbling crowd.

"Don't let them get away. Stop them, somebody!" Pamphilus screamed from the ground. A nasty red lump had appeared on his head.

Pip took her chance and charged towards the tent, leaping over the fallen Pamphilus as she did so. Suddenly, a voice behind her bellowed;

"There he is! That's the Greek boy we just bought. Marcus, get a hold of him. Stop him at once!" Gaius yelled.

Two large hands clamped themselves onto Pip's shoulders, pinning her to the spot. By now, the ground had stopped shaking and the crowd had stopped shrieking.

"The little rascal thought he could make a run for it, did he? Not so fast, my boy. I've just paid seven hundred for you, little scoundrel. I hope you're not going to make me regret it. Shows he's got spirit though, eh Marcus? Take him home, will you? I still have business to attend to." Gaius' voice trailed off as he set off towards home. The heavy hands on Pip's shoulders powerfully turned her around. She was face to face with her captor.

Seven

Pip tried to squirm away but the huge hands on her shoulders held her tight. She looked up into the giant's face. It was the man she'd seen with the children outside the House of Venus.

"Listen, mate, you're lucky Gaius didn't give you the lash. Stop wriggling," he said.

"But my mum," Pip said, "I have to…" she tried to pull away again. She lashed out with her feet but he was too big and strong to notice.

"Now look," Marcus said, steering her over to a stone bench, through a sea of roasted chickpeas from an overturned snack cart. "Sit here and let me tell you something." He pushed her onto the bench.

"I know exactly what it's like. You've been torn from your family. You miss them, eh? Especially your mum. It's hard. I know it's hard, but you'll learn to live with the grief. This is your life now."

"You can't take me; you don't understand." The full horror of the situation began to dawn on Pip.

"But I do understand. I understand more than you know. I'm from England originally, London. Have you heard of London? I was with my mum on the battlefield there, fighting this lot, these Romans." Marcus stopped to wave his hands in a giant circle. "We were fighting with Boudica. You heard of her?" Pip nodded. "Anyway, MY mum, she was slain RIGHT before my eyes. Right in front of me. Killed. Chopped down. Dead.

Do you know what happened then? I didn't even have time to think, let alone cry. I was grabbed by a Roman soldier, kept in their camp for a few months, then shipped off to Rome. I was worked like a dog in the fields for a few years then I was sold to Mr Gaius." Marcus paused and bent down to wipe a tear from Pip's cheek with his thumb. He looked into her face then said gently,

"This isn't the place for tears, mate. You need to learn that now. Gaius isn't one of the bad ones but see these scars on my arms and legs? I got those when I was about your age. It's best for you if you just accept your fate. You're from Greece, right? It's not so different here. You'll soon pick things up. It's a good household, one of the best in town. Gaius Ambustus is a rich man. He can be strict sometimes but he's willing to give you a chance. Most slave owners would have beaten you half to death for trying to run away. What's your name, fellah?"

"Pip, my name is Pip and I'm not a…"

"Pleased to meet you, mate." The big man took Pip's arm and shook it at the wrist. "I'm Marcus, chief slave of the Ambustus household; pleased to make your acquaintance." He made a short bow, making Pip laugh a little.

"Pip's a good name, short and sweet. I like it. And to be honest, mate, you ARE a bit of a pipsqueak. They must have starved you since Gaius picked you out. He said you were a sturdy-looking little lad. We'll have to see about fattening you up." He looked down at her. There was kindness in his gaze. "We have to get going now; there's work to be done. Just remember, there's no use in running away. Accept your fate."

With one hand on her shoulder, Marcus guided Pip out of the forum grounds and into the town. They passed through the main streets and stopped at the bakery, the one Pip had seen the day before when she had been free.

"I bet you're hungry. Hey, Rufus!" Marcus slapped the baker on the back. "Give me one of those loaves for my new boy. He needs feeding up. Look at him. He's skin and bone."

The baker handed Marcus one of the round loaves from the display.

"I've only just built this lot up again since the earth tremor. Had to dust them down a bit."

"Can you put it on the account? Thanks, mate. See you tomorrow for the household order, and Rufus," Marcus laughed, "no burnt ones this time." He turned to Pip, "You need to watch him, young Pip me lad. He hides the burnt ones at the bottom of the basket."

The baker smiled as Pip and Marcus turned away.

"Here, get your gnashers round this." Marcus broke a huge chunk of bread from the loaf and handed it to Pip. It smelled delicious and she ate greedily.

"My, my, have they not fed you since Athens? That slave trader is a sly devil, always doing things on the cheap. Some of his slaves have been known to starve to death on the journey over. Anyway, you're no use to us as a bag of skin and bone. Gaius always says 'a hungry slave is a useless slave'."

Marcus broke off another chunk of bread and handed it to Pip. She ate it as they walked. Marcus went on;

"Let me fill you in a bit, kid. Gaius, our master, makes his money from fish sauce. Sounds funny, eh? You must have heard of our sauce over in Greece. We send it all over the world. Anyway, every day, we fetch fresh fish from the harbour and carry it on the mule's back to the workshop by the river."

Pip was finding it difficult to concentrate on what Marcus was saying to her. She was wondering where her mum was.

"Do you know Octavius?" she interrupted.

"What?"

"The farmer. The one who bought a slave at the auction today."

"Yes, I know Octavius, he's a friend of the family. You need to watch him; he's a nasty piece of work. What's the matter? You look worried."

"Oh, nothing. I was just wondering. Tell me more about the fish sauce." She had to hide her interest in the farmer.

"So, the guys in the workshop ferment the fish in barrels. I swear their noses are made out of clay. Boy, the stench in there is enough to turn your stomach inside out. It's amazing that it tastes so good when it smells so bad. We have a secret ingredient, young Pip. Stick around and you might get to find out what it is."

Pip had no intention of sticking around if she could help it. She wished Mrs Higgins was there to help her hatch an escape plan. Marcus was still talking about fish sauce;

"Gaius' son, Lucius, you'll meet him later. He had a terrible earache last year. The pain was driving him doo-lally. He was howling like a stuck pig. Do you know what we did? We held him down and poured some fish sauce down his lughole. He smelled a bit rotten for a day or two but it as sure as Hades fixed his ear."

Marcus turned Pip onto the Via dell'Abbondanza. They walked past the Stabian Baths and just after they passed the House of Venus, Marcus stopped suddenly.

"Look, kid, can you see it? This is our house," he declared proudly. He marched Pip up the entrance. A fishy aroma curled up her nostrils like smoke. She pinched her nose.

"Oh, don't mind the smell, you'll soon get used to it. It clings to your tunic, mind. People usually know I'm on my way before I arrive because of the stink on my tunic."

"The house next door," Pip said, "The House of Venus."

"What about it?"

"Didn't someone break into it recently?" Pip asked.

"How do you know about that?" Marcus asked, scratching his chin.

"What will happen to the woman they caught?"

"She's lucky to still be in one piece that one. Jupiter knows how she escaped a flogging. Anyway, the authorities sold her to the slave dealer and Octavius bought her. He said he had plans for her. I have no idea what he's up to, but it's probably 'orrible."

"When will you know?"

"Know what, mate?" Marcus was becoming irritated.

"What his plans are with the woman."

"Look here, Pip. Never you mind. It's none of your business. THIS household is your business." He looked down at Pip and saw that she was upset. He tousled her hair.

"Ah, I think I understand now. You spent some time with her with the other slaves at the auction? Did she tell you a sob story?"

"No," Pip said. "She was kind to me, that's all. I'm worried Octavius will treat her badly."

"Octavius treats all his slaves badly, but don't you worry about that. You'll be fine here. Gaius isn't cruel like Octavius."

Pip flinched. Marcus put his hand on her shoulders and spoke gravely;

"Snap out of it, Pip." He gave her a gentle shake. "Come on, let's get you settled into the house. I have work to do."

Marcus ushered her through the door and past a porch area containing rows and rows of jars holding the family fish sauce. They walked along a passage leading to the domestic part of the house. Pip stopped dead.

"Admiring the mosaic, eh? I told you our master was rich. That thing cost a fortune and took months to finish."

Pip looked at the snarling dog straining on its leash. As she looked more closely, she could see that it was made up of tiny black and white stones. Its tongue was red. It looked so real it had startled her. She almost expected to hear it growl.

"Something to put burglars off, eh? Pity they haven't got one next door. It's ok, you can step on it. Come this way." He led her through a narrow passage and into a vast hall. She gasped. She had seen nothing like it before. The walls around the hall were painted vivid colours; solid blocks of reds, gold, greens and black. Some walls had intricate hunting scenes painted onto them. Marcus went on;

"See the pool in the middle? I tiled that myself. It collects rainwater which is vital these days since the wells have been drying up." Pip went over and dipped her fingers in the cool water. She looked up at the hole in the roof through which the water came and saw the bluest of skies.

"This is the family shrine," Marcus said, pointing to the corner of the room. "Bacchus is our special household God." Pip turned to face the shrine. In the middle of the shrine stood a statue of Bacchus riding a sleek and muscular panther.

"One of your jobs will be to make Bacchus shine. The more we worship him, the more he blesses Pompeii with our grape harvest, and you know what grapes make, don't you, Pip? That's right, wine. The family drink plenty of it, I can tell you."

"Octavius grows grapes, doesn't he? Does he also make wine?"

"What is it with you and Octavius?" Marcus said, "You ARE like a dog with a bone. But yes, Octavius grows the grapes and makes his own wine."

"Do you think he wanted that female slave to tread grapes to make his wine?" she asked.

"Oh no, I very much doubt it. He has loads of slaves already to do that for him. You can tell which ones; they have purple feet."

Pip thought of her mum with her feet dyed purple.

"No, if you ask me, he has something out of the ordinary planned for that slave. Something sinister, more than likely. Did she tell you her name?"

"Um…" Pip quickly thought of a Roman name, "Her name is Vesta."

"Goddess of home and hearth," Marcus said, "Though I doubt she'll get near Octavius' hearth. A fire pit maybe, but not his hearth." Pip shuddered. She wondered if it had been a good idea to come and rescue her mum. The task seemed impossible now she was actually here.

"It's usually busier in here," Marcus said looking round. "The kids must be playing out in the garden."

Pip brightened at the thought of having friends to confide in but what Marcus said next shattered those hopes.

"Be careful of those two; they're troublemakers, especially Lucius. They wield a lot of power with our master and mistress. They can get you the lash… or worse. If one of them slaps you, well, if Lucius slaps you, because it will be Lucius, just dig your nails into your palms. And remember, definitely no tears. The more you cry, the harder they beat you."

"Marcus, is that you?" a woman's voice called from upstairs.

"Yes, I've got someone here you might want to meet. I've got our new slave boy," Marcus shouted back.

"Wait, I'm coming down. I have his clothes." Quinta descended the stairs carrying a pile of white tunics and a pair of sandals. She joined them in the hall.

"So, you're our new boy. You've come all the way from Greece?"

"Yes, he's a bit rough round the edges but we'll sort him out in a week or two. He's already had one bid for freedom and a whinge and a cry when he was caught again. I think he'll settle down soon. He knows what side his loaf is oiled, don't you, mate?" Marcus ruffled Pip's hair.

Quinta crouched down onto her knees in front of Pip, took her hands gently and gave them a squeeze.

"Welcome to the household. And these are for you." She handed Pip the clothes. "Do you want to pop one on now and put the rest in your locker? I can tear up that old thing you've got on into rags for rubbing down the mule…"

"Don't be so soft with him," Marcus scolded, smiling. "You'll make a right wimp out of him."

Pip didn't want to get undressed. She still had on her swimsuit under her potato sack;

"It's ok, I'll change later," she said quietly. Nobody seemed concerned.

"He's missing his mum," Quinta said, "just like we missed ours. Anyway, I'm off to work. I have so much to do for Madam Decima." She swept away to the far end of the hall.

"Isn't she great?" Marcus beamed. "She'll be my wife when we're free. I can't wait. Right, where was I? Oh yes, there are eleven slaves in the household now you've arrived. All the others are out at the workshop or doing other chores for Gaius or Decima, our mistress."

"What's Decima like?" Pip asked.

"Well…" Marcus thought, "I'm sure there are worse mistresses in Rome. She can be a bit particular. Just do as she says and do it quickly. So, Gaius has suggested we start off teaching you the basics, you know, see what strengths and weaknesses you have. It's better for you if you stay in the household. The work is easier, and the plan is for you to take over from me when I get my freedom. What do you think, kiddo?"

"I'll try my best," Pip said.

"You will if you know what's good for you," was Marcus' reply. "There's a lot of work to do at the moment. There are some walls that need patching up because of the earth tremors."

"Because of Vesuvius?" Pip realised her mistake as soon as she'd said it.

"Oh, that old thing. Nothing to worry about there. Some silly superstitious people packed up and left, ooh, must be fifteen years ago now after the last big quake, but we're still alive, aren't we? I told you. We pray to Bacchus and he looks after us. Why would anyone want to leave?"

Pip bit her tongue, remembering Mrs Higgins' warning.

"In fact, the garden wall hasn't been mended properly since that quake. The little one earlier today didn't make it much worse. I don't think we'll get a bigger quake any time soon. The thing with the fountains is annoying though. They seem to be drying up. We're having to bring barrels from the river by mule. You can help with that, but I think over the next few days we'll ease you in with stuff around the home."

Pip looked up at Marcus and smiled weakly.

"Where will I sleep?" she asked, hoping for some time alone.

"I'll take you upstairs to the slaves' quarters," said Marcus as they climbed the stairs together.

"It can get a bit cramped when the fellas come home but you'll be as snug as a bug in a rug. More often than not, you'll sleep where you drop but if you have the chance to make it upstairs, you can sleep here on the floor."

They had entered a tiny room strewn with pieces of thin matting made from reeds. These were covered by thin, grubby blankets. There was only one proper solid bed by the far wall, onto which several wooden lockers had been attached. Pip thought the room smelled like a pigsty.

"I'm the boss up here, kid. That's my bed over there. When I'm not here, the boys might fight over it but I'm afraid, as the new kid in town, you're at the bottom of the heap."

Pip sighed as she looked around the dingy room. She couldn't imagine how it would feel with ten other people in it.

"Alright, kid, let's crack on. We need to start cleaning before the master gets home. He likes his place to be spotless. Find an empty locker for your new things and I'll see you downstairs."

Pip felt quite smart in her new white tunic. The sandals pinched a bit, but her feet had been hurting from treading on stones in the street. She put the other tunics away and raced down to the shrine. She handed her potato sack to Marcus.

"I'll give that to Quinta. Right, let's start in the kitchen. I can introduce you to the cook if he's about. I'm sure he'd appreciate another pair of hands. He's always moaning about having to clean the lav. That can be your first job."

Pip grimaced. Her quest to rescue her mum seemed to have put her right back at square one but this time skivvying for different people a long way from home.

Eight

"Ah, that's where you've been hiding, Spurius. I have the new slave boy here. I'm showing him the ropes."

Marcus and Pip had walked through the ornate hallway, past several other rooms separated by painted wooden screens. They had turned right into what Pip assumed was the kitchen. It was rather cramped. She banged her head on some pots and pans that hung from the ceiling.

At the far end of the kitchen, a fat man sat on a wooden bench. His face was flushed, and he was grimacing.

"This is Pip, Spurius. I thought we'd throw him in at the deep end, starting with the latrines," Marcus said.

"Excellent, excellent. What better time to learn? Pass me the sponge, boy," Spurius said beckoning Pip over.

Marcus prodded her in the direction of a utensil jar at Spurius' feet.

"Don't worry, matey, you don't have to wipe my backside, just pass the damned thing to me," Spurius said laughing.

Pip lifted one of the sticks from the jar and handed it to the cook. A sponge was attached to the end of the stick with twine. Drops of dirty water dribbled from it onto the floor. He took it from her. Pip turned away.

"Feeling queasy, eh, boy?" Spurius laughed again, "I suppose you've never pooped before."

"Not in a kitchen, no," Pip replied, still facing the wall, "and certainly not with an audience."

"That's unusual, considering you're a slave. Kept in solitary all your life, were you? Anyway, thank Jupiter there's a lav here at all and you don't have to join the queue for the public ones in town. There's nothing worse than smelling your neighbours' droppings while they're being dropped, I can tell you. This place is pure luxury."

"Don't be too hard on him, Spurius," said Marcus. "He's freshly plucked from his mother's bosom. Aren't you, Pip?" He approached her and tousled her hair roughly. He explained to Spurius;

"He arrived from Greece only this morning. There was uproar at the forum. I suppose you felt the earthquake. Three of the slaves made a dash for it. They've all been caught now, Pip included."

"Oh? Well, I never." Spurius had finished with the sponge. He stood up and rearranged his tunic. Marcus went on;

"The other two weren't as lucky as our little chap. They both had a public flogging. Nothing too harsh. I don't suppose the slave trader wants damaged goods but I'm sure their scars will be a permanent reminder to them. Running away is ALWAYS a bad idea."

"Well, well, "Spurius mused. "Can't blame them for wanting to be free, can you? I must admit, I used to think about doing a runner when I was younger but where is there to run to?" He curled his moustache around his fingers as he spoke. His words reminded Pip of the predicament she was in. He turned to her with a smile that split his fat red face in two, exposing blackened teeth.

"Let's get the formalities out of the way, shall we?" he said, grabbing her by the shoulders. "Spurius is my name. I'm the chief cook and bottle-washer, gardener, emptier of cesspits, childminder and general dog's body. Get the picture?" He stuck his plump hand out towards Pip in order to shake hers.

Spurius' hand was filthy and Pip hesitated.

"Come on, boy," he said grasping her wrist and pumping her arm vigorously. "Pleased to meet you." Once he'd let go, Pip tried to wipe herself discreetly on her tunic.

"So, my boy, the latrines. Here's the deal. Every morning, it's your job to collect all the chamber pots from the sleeping areas. Fetch Madam Decima's first and empty it into here. She gets cross if her room smells of stale piss. Not for now though, as she's staying with her mother in Naples."

Marcus assisted by lifting the wooden lid from the toilet bench, showing Pip the tiled slope leading to, as Spurius explained, the cesspit below. Pip was overcome by the smell. She held her nose.

"If anything sticks to the sides, fetch some water from the barrel, there's not much in the well at the moment, and give it a scrub with the sponge here."

Pip realised he meant the sponge on the stick he'd just used to wipe his bottom.

"Alright, Spurius, I can see you're going to make a good team," Marcus interrupted. "Can I leave Pip with you? I have to meet Gaius in town. Make sure he doesn't run away, PLEASE."

"Don't worry, boss, he'll be safe with me," said Spurius. Marcus smiled and left the kitchen, bending low to avoid bashing his head on the pots and pans.

"Right, Pip, there's a lot to do this afternoon," said Spurius, rubbing his hands together. "The guys will be home from the workshop soon and they need feeding. Those two brats in the garden have been whining that they're hungry too. I'll take you to meet them." Spurius picked up a tray of food from the kitchen worktop. He gave it to her to carry.

"Do you know Octavius?" Pip asked, taking the tray from him.

"What an odd question. Yes, I do know Octavius. I wish I didn't, mind. Why do you ask?"

"Oh," Pip thought for a second then said, "I've just heard what fabulous wine he makes."

"Yes, he does make fabulous wine and he drinks a fair amount of it himself. That's why his nose is purple. He's coming here for dinner very soon. If I was a brave man, Pip, my lad, I'd add some hemlock to his honey."

The cook wiped his hands on his apron and escorted Pip from the cluttered kitchen. They emerged through a narrow corridor that led to a large green curtain. Pip could hear the high-pitched chatter of children squabbling as Spurius swished the curtain aside and pushed her out into the garden.

Pip glanced around. The garden was enclosed by painted walls with covered walkways around the edges. Carved columns marked the corners. How funny to have a garden within the house, she thought.

Her eyes were drawn to the centre of the garden, where an aisle had been made of flowerbeds and a series of small water fountains ran in parallel. The fountains were all dry.

Everything in the garden was arranged in long rows, leading towards a life-size marble statue of Bacchus. He held aloft a bunch of grapes and lowered them playfully into his mouth.

"Those are the children of the household, Pip," said Spurius as they made their way down the garden, "Lucius and his little sister Tiberia."

Pip saw the children she'd seen outside the House of Venus. They started to chase each other around the statue.

"Give him to me. Give him to me NOW!" screamed Tiberia.

"I shan't. I'm keeping him. He's mine now and I'm going to roast him and eat him."

"But he's mine. You got bored of yours. It's not FAIR!"

"Yes, but mine died and I'm the oldest and you're just a girl, so I'm taking this one."

"Yours died because you forgot to give him water," said Tiberia. She reached up and snatched the small clay pot Lucius was clutching tightly to his chest, knocking it out of his hands. The pot fell to the floor and smashed. The dormouse, startled into wakefulness and freed from its clay chamber, meandered under a bush unseen by the arguing children.

"Children, children, please. What's all the commotion?" Spurius asked.

"Lucius killed his mouse and then tried to steal mine and he broke the pot and now the mouse has escaped," gabbled Tiberia without pausing for breath.

"Oh, never mind that now; it's only a dormouse. If you ask Octavius nicely, I'm sure he'll give you another one. Have you been feeding the peacock? He needs to be nice and plump. He'll take raisins from your hand if you're quiet."

"Lucius scared the peacock away. He pulled a feather out of his tail for Mummy's hair and I've not seen him since," Tiberia said.

Having only just noticed Pip's presence, Lucius quickly changed the subject.

"Who is THAT?" he demanded, jabbing the air with his finger.

"Lucius, Tiberia, I'd like you both to meet our new slave boy. His name is Pip and he's come all the way from Athens to work for us. Be nice to him, PLEASE. Pip, put the children's tray on that bench. That's it. It's time for their dinner." Lucius ignored the food.

"Our new slave, is he?" he mocked, walking slowly towards Pip, "He looks like a girl. Why did Daddy buy such a rubbish-looking slave? Furthermore, Spurius, he can't be allowed to keep his own name. WE need to give him one. Let's see," he said, scratching his chin, "I'm going to name him Porcus because he looks, and indeed SMELLS like a pig. Welcome to the household, Porcus."

Pip ignored Lucius. She picked up the sleepy dormouse she'd seen crawl under the bush and handed it to Tiberia. "Be gentle with it," she said, smiling at the little girl, "It's tiny and quite delicate. I had a mouse as a pet once; I can help you look after it."

Tiberia thanked her and placed the mouse delicately in her tunic pocket.

Lucius was furious. He marched up to Pip.

"HOW DARE YOU?" he screamed in her face, "How dare ANY slave in MY daddy's household behave in such a way? You're a SLAVE!" he yelled, spittle forming at the corners of his mouth, "and slaves don't do ANYTHING unless a proper citizen tells them to do it!"

"Is that right?" Pip said, looking down at Lucius. His face had turned a deep shade of purple. Lucius didn't bother to answer. He raised his right hand and cuffed Pip's ear, sending her reeling into a small potted laurel tree.

"That's enough, Master Lucius," said the cook. He grabbed hold of Pip and pulled her to her feet, "Eat your meal quietly, you two; we have work to do."

Pip's ear was stinging and she longed to retaliate but sense got the better of her. Spurius ushered her out of the garden and back into the kitchen.

"How could you be so stupid?" He grabbed her tunic at the neck and shook her. "You REALLY are playing with fire and you've only been here five minutes. That boy, nasty specimen that he is, could have you whipped and thrown out on your ear; or much, much worse." He let go of her.

"I'm sorry, Spurius, I forgot."

"Forgot what? That you are a slave? Now listen here, I'm only telling you this because I like you. These people own us. Do you understand? They feed us and they shelter us, but they can beat us and even kill us without a thought. PLEASE remember this."

"Yes, I've been very stupid," Pip said. She had to run away. That was all there was to it. She'd leave that night. She'd sneak out when everyone else was asleep. She had to get to her mother and take her home before something terrible happened. Spurius smiled and ruffled her hair.

"That's better, now help me with this lot." Spurius turned to the workbench and began to assemble food onto trays. "Each man has a loaf, a chunk of this cheese here, cut into triangles. Got it? Two tomatoes, a bowl of olive oil, four figs and half a bottle of wine to dilute with this big jug of water. It's a shame we can't dish out some of our fish sauce, but the men are sick of the stuff."

"Did Octavius make that wine?" Pip asked.

"Nah," said the cook, "This is just cheap plonk. What's this obsession with Octavius anyway?"

"Oh, I'm just curious," Pip said. "Do his slaves live in the farmhouse with him? Like we do with Gaius' family, I mean."

"I doubt it. He probably chains them up in an outhouse," Spurius said. "Most of his slaves he uses on the land. He probably has one house slave, maybe a cook, but they never had children and Octavius takes care of his own business.

Marcus does a lot of work for our master's business and Fortuna does our master's accounts. Octavius, on the other hand, sorts out his own business affairs."

"Fortuna?" Pip asked.

"Yes, Fortuna is her name; that's all you need to know."

"Why?"

"I don't like saying her name more than once, that's all."

"But why not?"

"Stop with all the questions, would you?" Spurius softened; "Alright, she's into magic and things. She used to be a slave in the Faustus family, a few years ago now. They discovered that she had 'the gift' shall we say."

"What sort of gift?"

"She is able to see things that ordinary mortals cannot; in livers mainly. She's a haruspicina."

"A what?"

"She has an uncanny flair for hepatoscopy."

"Oh, that sounds a bit gruesome; not human livers, I hope."

"I wouldn't put it past her but no, animal livers as far as I am aware." Pip was intrigued and asked, "So why is she doing our family's accounts?"

"She made a lot of money from the Faustus family and bought her freedom. She is known to have made many clever investments and word got out. Let's just say she has many talents. Just watch yourself with her or she might put a spell on you or make you drink one of her magic potions… But enough chat. Take these trays up to the slaves' quarters then you can come down and eat. You must be hungry."

Pip nodded and did as she was told. It took her four trips past Quinta who was still busy in the hall with needlework. All the while she thought about her impending escape. She didn't think it would be too difficult. The front door wasn't locked, and she already knew where Octavius lived. She could run there in half an hour or so, find the outhouse where her mum was being kept, then once reunited, they could quickly dash to the pool together. Simple.

She was tired and hungry when she returned to the kitchen.

"Here you go, kid," said the cook, placing a smaller version of the men's meal in front of her. "Have a feast on this. A proper meal for a proper day's work. We'll make a man of you in time, my boy."

If only he knew, Pip thought as she ate greedily. If the family found out she was a girl, she would be in serious trouble. Still, there was no need to worry about that now. She'd be free of the place by midnight.

68

"I think you should go and lie in the arms of Morpheus, Pip," Spurius said. "You look done-in."

"What do you mean?"

"You know Morpheus. He's one of YOUR gods. Son of Hypnos? God of dreams? I'm not just a pretty face you know. I could have been a scholar if I'd not been born into slavery. Go upstairs and have a sleep is what I'm saying. You're no more use to me today. You're a good kid; I'm glad you're here to help."

"Thanks, Spurius," Pip said, and she meant it. She liked the fat cook with his happy red face and silly moustache. She left the kitchen saying 'goodnight' to Quinta as she passed her again in the hall.

She climbed the stairs and fell onto the reed bed in the corner of the slaves' room nearest the door so she could escape easily when the time came. The men were not yet back from the workshop and the food she had brought up remained un-eaten on the trays.

Pip pulled the thin grey blanket over her head and got as comfortable as she could on the scratchy mattress.

She slept for a few hours before a fishy aroma crept into her dreams. She felt the floor under her mattress vibrate, gently shaking her awake. She didn't move a muscle but very gingerly opened one eye.

"Hey, look guys, this must be the new slave boy. They were right enough, he's a bit of a pipsqueak."

A group of men had stomped loudly into the room and were tucking into the food and wine.

"As long as he doesn't take up too much space, that's fine by me," said another of the slaves, wiping oil from his chin with the back of his hand.

"He must be tired, I reckon, sleeping through this din. I hear he gave them a bit of a headache at the slave auction, trying to make a run for it."

"Good for him," another man chipped in. "Shows he's got guts. Small and tough, like a weasel," said another man. He threw a piece of bread at Pip's head. She remained still, even though it stung.

The men soon forgot about Pip. They carried on eating and drinking until they too bedded down for the night. Once the lamps went out, Pip rolled over onto her back and opened her eyes, ready to rise and creep out of the room. Two men were still talking, one of whom was lying in Marcus' big bed. That meant he must be in town for the night. Escaping would be easier with Marcus away.

Pip waited and waited. Eventually, she closed her eyes. All her muscles relaxed while she waited but the men were still whispering. Soon she was in a half-dream. Her mother's face, its features indistinct, hovered over her and planted a goodnight kiss on her forehead. The kiss sent Pip into a deep, deep sleep.

Nine

A loud snore woke Pip up. She opened her eyes and blinked. The room was too dark even for shadows. She was annoyed with herself for having fallen asleep; she should have been away by now. She rolled over very carefully and raised herself up on her elbows. There was a sleeping body next to her. One of the men must have rolled from his mattress onto hers. She nudged him away, scrambled to her feet and slid out of the room.

Pip tiptoed down the stairs and into the hall. A lamp was burning weakly on the shrine. She made her way past the pool and picked up the lamp. She walked into the kitchen, used the loo and washed her hands and face in the water barrel. She was hungry. She tore some bread from a loaf on the counter and ate hurriedly.

Before she left the kitchen, she blew out the flame of the lamp she was carrying. She emerged into the hallway and peered around. It was still very dark. She tiptoed over to the door and reached for the handle;

"Not so fast!" a reedy voice called from behind her. She turned to face Lucius, his features grotesque in the light as he held a lamp under his chin.

"Going somewhere, are you? Hmm…?" he taunted, his breath warm and pungent in her face. "Not now you're not. I've caught you red-handed." Pip turned again and lunged for the door handle, but Lucius had grabbed the hem of her tunic and yanked her backwards. Pip lost her footing and stumbled into him, knocking the boy onto his back. She landed on top of him. He let out an 'oof'.

"What's all this commotion?" Marcus had heard the disturbance and had come to investigate. Lucius was struggling to breathe under Pip's weight.

"This… wretch… this wretched slave… was… running away…"

"That's not true," Pip countered. "It was dark and I was looking for the kitchen. My lamp had gone out, see? I made a wrong turning, that's all." She could feel Lucius writhing under her and she pressed down harder on him.

"Well, that's understandable, mate. Pip's new here and doesn't know his way around yet. Come on, get up, both of you," Marcus said. Pip sprang up. Lucius gave another 'oof' as her weight lifted from his lungs. He staggered to his feet. "I'm watching you, Porcus," he said under his breath before stomping off to his bedroom.

Marcus placed his hands on Pip's shoulders and steered her back through the hallway. Instead of turning her into the kitchen, he led her out to the garden.

"I'm glad you're up early. I have a little job for you to do. The mule needs mucking out. The stench from her stable is getting unbearable. That's bound to spoil the family's dinner party tomorrow. Madam Decima will be irate if anything ruins her special day. You met Dentata the other day, didn't you? Watch out for her great big teeth; you don't want a nip, and also, watch her back end. She's rather fond of launching Lucius into the air with those hoofs of hers.

You'll find a spade and a broom in the shed next to the stable and PLEASE keep out of that boy's way. I think he's got it in for you."

Marcus hurried back towards the house and Pip turned the handle on the stable door. It was pitch black inside. Marcus was right, the smell was awful. She stepped in and split the stable door to let in some light.

"Hello, Pip. I've been expecting you." Pip nearly jumped out of her skin. When her eyes had become accustomed to the poor light, she saw Dentata the mule gazing at her. Pip was confused and looked around to see if anyone else was in the stable with her.

"Was that you?" she asked the mule.

"Maybe there's someone else hiding in the straw," Dentata said.

"Oh…," Pip stuttered. "How do you know my name? And how come you can talk?"

72

"Well, here's the thing," the mule began, "I met your mother recently. She was spying on the Satri house and came over to give me a pat. She looked nervous, like a fish out of water. She certainly looked like she didn't belong here and it made me wonder if old Toothless had been recruiting the needy again. I took pity on her and we got chatting. Have a look under the straw there. She hid some stuff."

Pip rummaged around in the banks of straw piled up against the stable walls. Her hands fell on something big and round and made of metal. She felt around its edge;

"Is this what I think it is?"

"That depends what you think it is," the mule replied sagely. "If you think it's a TV set, you'd be wrong." Pip gave a tug and heaved the gladiator's shield from the straw. Its diameter spanned the width of both her arms, "Wow," she whistled. "How did she manage to pinch this without being seen?"

"It was tricky, very tricky, but I gave her a hand, well, hoof, I gave her four hoofs actually."

"I'm impressed."

"Well, yes, she was doing very well indeed until she was caught in the House of Venus. There's loads more stuff there but never mind that for now. Your mum told me about the plan they'd hatched together, her and Harriet, for you to come and fetch her if things went wrong. Well, things certainly DID go wrong…"

Pip covered up the treasure.

"How come you can talk?" she asked again.

"I suffered the same fate as your friend Mrs Higgins, though, of course, she was Harriet Nash when we were friends," the mule said, shifting her weight onto her other front hoof. "Old Toothless sent me to Pompeii after Harriet returned in her murine state. We're obviously cut from the same cloth, her and I, because I couldn't bear to keep my mouth shut about the impending volcanic eruption.

I managed to encourage a few people, who did leave town, but I got my timing wrong. I put the wrong year into the dial. AD 69 I put in. I didn't have my specs on. So, I was blabbing about it far too

73

soon. Anyway, when I gave my warning, a mule passed in the street and well, you can guess the rest."

"So, you've been here for ten years?"

"Just over ten, yes. It's not much fun being a mule, I can tell you."

"No, I bet. Who were you to Toothless? What's your real name?"

"I'm Jane Jones, a friend of Harriet, Toothless' sister as I'm sure you know her to be. We were at university together and I wanted to start my PhD but didn't have any funding. Toothless came up with this grand idea and I desperately wanted my doctorate. I'm a very keen philosopher, or I was, so here I am."

"That's so tragic," Pip said, stroking the mule under her forelock.

"Yes, I should have known it was a bad idea, especially with Harriet gone. How is she, by the way?"

"She's fine, I hope. I wanted her to come with me, but she said she was too old. I miss her."

"Toothless didn't tell her then?"

"Tell her what?" Pip scratched her chin.

"If the animal that you have become dies of unnatural causes then you return to human form."

"Oh…!" Pip was stunned. "So, Mrs Higgins has spent all these years being a mouse when she could have been Harriet again? The Harriet you knew, Harriet Nash?"

"Yes," said the mule, "but she would have posed a threat to Toothless and Bladderwash. She'd have exposed their evil ways, so they made sure she could never be human again. They'll be waiting for her to die of old age. Think about it. They managed to trap and kill a few of her children but never her. They very cleverly kept her safe."

"And you?" Pip asked. "How come you're still a mule?"

"My dear girl, have a good hard feel of my head. Just where you're stroking. Can you feel how thick it is? I've tried all sorts, trust me. I've walloped my head against the Temple of Apollo so many times, I'm amazed it's still standing. I've bashed down columns and dented walls, but my head has remained intact. I've thrown myself into the sea, to be pulled out by fishermen. I've eaten poison ivy, AND the stuff they leave out to poison the foxes, but a mule's stomach seems to be impervious to every nasty thing I could think of."

"There must be something we can do."

"Well, yes, there is. I've had to use my brain a little. I've been limping and struggling under the loads they've been giving me. On purpose, you see? They don't want a useless beast. They will just think I'm getting past my sell-by date. I've been with the family for ten years; they'll think I've had my day."

"But why should you die?" Pip was puzzled.

"Oh, they're sending the slaughterman round later this week. They'll want to turn me into food for the slaves who work in the mines, or dog food maybe; your guess is as good as mine. Tiberia will be distraught, of course. I think I'm her only friend. That stupid brother of hers is a constant torment to her."

"It all sounds terribly grisly."

'Yes, it will be. But I suppose the pain will be bearable if I know I'll be returning to my original state."

"When you're back to your old self, you can come home with my mum and me. As soon as I've rescued her, of course," Pip said. "In fact, you can help me rescue her. You know where she is, don't you? She's being held by Octavius the farmer. I think she's locked in one of his outhouses."

"I was hoping you'd say that," Dentata replied. "I'd love to help you find Carrie AND it will be such a relief to get back home. I can't wait to get my old teeth back." The mule curled back her lips showing a snaggled row of enormous yellow teeth. Pip laughed;

"I suppose I'd better get on with cleaning your stable then, you dirty old thing."

"Ah," replied her new friend, "I got used to standing knee-high in my own dung many years ago."

Pip and Dentata were disturbed by a knock on the stable door. Pip opened it and saw Tiberia standing outside with tears rolling down her cheeks. The little girl rushed in and threw her arms around the mule.

"Daddy said they are going to have you killed. I won't let them. I won't!" she sobbed. Dentata gave a small whinny and scraped her hoof along the stable floor. She nuzzled Tiberia with her nose. Pip tried to be grown-up about it all.

"Sometimes we have to be kind to animals by putting them to sleep," she said, "to end their suffering."

"But she isn't suffering. Look at her. She's not in pain, she's just getting a bit too old for working. I love her so much. She's my only friend. Well, her and Marcus. I come here every day to see her. I steal food for her from the kitchen. How can Daddy say he's going to kill her? It's just horrible. Why can't we keep her and get another mule? They can share the stable. Couldn't they?"

"Some people only see animals as possessions, Tiberia. They don't realise they feel things like we do, especially Dentata here."

"I'm not going to let them do it. I'm really not."

"I tell you what," Pip said, "why don't you put a braid in Dentata's forelock? Take that one from your own hair and put it in hers. Make her feel special while I clean out all the muck."

"Yes, that's a good idea. I'll make her feel special, but I'm going to protect her, I really am."

Pip began her work. She took countless buckets of muck from the stable through the door leading onto the street and dumped it in the gutter. When she'd finished and put down some fresh straw for bedding, Dentata's stable was as clean as a whistle and the mule had a pretty plait in her forelock, tied with a dark green ribbon.

"She looks lovely," Pip said. "Let's go into the house. You must be hungry." They both patted the mule goodbye and Tiberia took Pip's rather grubby hand and they made their way into the kitchen where Marcus was talking to Spurius the cook.

"Yes, I'll take Pip up to the farm this afternoon and collect the food for the dinner tomorrow night. I hope Octavius has everything ready." Pip's ears pricked up.

"I'll say one thing for the evil nincompoop, he DOES grow the best produce in all of Rome," Spurius said, twiddling his moustache. Marcus noticed Pip and Tiberia.

"Ah, hello you two. Are you after some food?" He fetched two plates and heaped them with bread, cheese and tomatoes. "Tuck in then, you'll be coming on some errands with me later. Where's your brother, Tiberia?"

"He's having his lessons," she said through a mouthful of tomato. "Greek, I think."

"Ah, such a beautiful language," Marcus said, puffing out his chest with mock pomposity. "So dignified. Would you like to pop in and give them a hand, Pip my lad? With it being your native tongue and all?"

"No, thank you," she replied. Marcus tousled her hair and grinned.

"Hurry up and finish that lot then. I'll get the mule ready with the cart. I hope she'll manage the journey today; she's been limping badly. She should really be rested until the slaughterman comes but there's so much work to do."

"I won't let you do that," Tiberia shouted. "I won't let you kill her." Tears began to fall down her cheeks again. She climbed down from her stool and started to sob.

"Come on, Miss Tiberia," Spurius said. "They'll get another one soon enough. You can give him the bread you steal from my kitchen. I know all about it. I've seen you pinching it to take to Dentata," he said grinning.

"A new mule won't be the same. I love Dentata; she's my best friend."

"Come now, don't cry," Marcus said, leading the little girl out of the kitchen. "Sometimes we have to put up with things we don't like. We just have to. It's the way of the world."

Pip finished her lunch and left the house by the front door. Marcus was waiting for her, holding Dentata's harness.

"Jump up into the back," he said, pointing at the cart. "There's some rags in the bottom. Make it comfy."

Pip grabbed the side of the cart and vaulted over. She bunched up some rags to kneel on and held on to the front of the cart as Marcus clicked the mule on towards the farm. Dentata stumbled a few times and Pip smiled to herself, knowing she was doing it on purpose.

"She seems to know the way," she said.

"Aye, the old girl's been up to Octavius' farm a thousand times," Marcus said. "Her time is coming to an end though, young Pip. She's getting too long in the tooth for working now."

The cart left the city at the Sarno Gate and joined the path Pip had used to get to Pompeii from her pool.

"Do you still miss your mum?" Pip asked.

"Every day," Marcus said. "There isn't a day that goes by when I don't think about her and what they did to her. It breaks my heart."

"I'm sorry, Marcus."

"What about your mum? What was she like?"

"Is she like, you mean? I've not seen her properly for a very long time. She had to leave me with a friend when she went away but I hope to see her again very soon."

"Really?" Marcus sounded surprised and turned to look at her. "I suppose it's good to stay positive when you find yourself in our predicament but sometimes it pays to be realistic." He turned back to face the road.

They had reached Octavius' farm. Without prompting, Dentata turned into the driveway that led into a large courtyard flagged by outhouses. Pip jumped down from the cart. Marcus called over to a slave who was sweeping spilled grain from the ground;

"Alright, mate. Can you let the boss know we're here? We've come from Master Gaius. For our order?"

The slave ran up to the house and disappeared inside. Marcus and Pip waited. Pip drew circles in the dust with her big toe.

"Ah, hello, Marcus." Octavius came along in a swoosh of purple robes. "Who is this you've brought with you? Is he pig feed? He doesn't look up to much." He stepped up to Pip and peered in her face.

"Have we met before? You look familiar." He peered more closely; "Yes, I'm CERTAIN we've met before. Mind you, Valentina says my eyesight's going, along with most of my hair sadly." He raised his right hand and rubbed his bald pate.

"This is our new household slave, sir," Marcus interrupted, trying to hide his irritation. He couldn't stand Octavius. "We've come to

78

collect the order for Madam Decima's dinner party. The family are looking forward to seeing you both tomorrow night."

"Well, it's nice to know I'll be contributing to the dinner. I hope that twit of a cook doesn't spoil my fine goods. I think he steals most of it and eats it himself, judging by the size of his belly."

"I'm sure Spurius tastes some of his dishes before he serves them, sir, just to make sure he's done things to perfection."

"Be that as it may, he's still a fat oaf. Speaking of slaves, did Gaius tell you about my new purchase? The woman caught trying to rob the House of Venus?"

"Yes, sir, he did," Marcus said. Pip felt a cold chill run through her.

"Well, come over here. Yes, you too; the runt can come," he said, pointing at Pip. "She's quite far away. In the field past the sheep. Can you see her? That's the rotten cat burglar. I'm training her up."

Pip and Marcus left the side of the cart. Marcus leant on the fence separating the courtyard from the meadow. He stared with Pip at two figures in the distance. They were both wielding sticks.

"What are you training her up for?" Marcus asked, laughing.

"She's going to be a gladiator, Marcus," Octavius said. "She's going to be in a fight to the death."

Ten

"Who will she be fighting, Mr Octavius, sir?" Pip tugged at the sleeves of the farmer's purple robe.

"Get your hands off me, PLEASE," he said, swatting her away. "Do YOU want to fight her to the death? You might just be a good match. There's a certain similarity between you and her. Were you whelped by the same mangy cur?"

"Will she be fighting a proper gladiator? You must tell me, please!" Pip was close to tears.

"That's enough now, Pip. Stop pestering Mr Octavius," Marcus said, steering her away from the meadow fence. Pip craned her neck to look behind at her mother, who was making clacking noises with a wooden sword against that of a farmhand.

"What made you think of that, sir? What gave you the idea?" Marcus asked, his hands still guiding Pip away from the farmer.

"She had my purple brooch on her, the thieving witch. NOBODY steals from me and doesn't live to regret it. This was the perfect punishment. Actually, between you and me, I will be having a flutter on this one. The farmer up the road owns an injured ex-gladiator. Do you remember Crispus? The one who lost his arm in a lion's mouth? Anyway, I bet him my woman could beat his maimed slave in a fight to the death."

"Bit unfair, isn't it? Even though he does only have one arm. He's a big lad, old Crispus, AND he's a trained fighter. Doesn't seem fair at all," Marcus said.

"Well, my dear Marcus, she should have thought about that, shouldn't she? And, what better entertainment is there than watching slaves take pieces out of each other? It's even more fun than throwing them to hungry beasts."

"With respect, sir, you are forgetting that I am also a slave," Marcus said, his face darkening.

"You shouldn't be complaining anyway," Octavius ignored him. "It'll be more bums on seats for your Master. He's hosting the games this year, is he not? The amphitheatre will be packed to the rafters. The graffiti is already daubed all over town; 'Malefica, that's what I've named her, Malefica versus One-Armed Crispus'." Octavius rubbed his hands together.

Marcus was angry; "What you say about any slave, you say about me too. Would you enjoy seeing ME hacked to pieces by a gladiator's sword?"

"Now, now, let's not upset ourselves. You know as well as I do that there are slaves and there are SLAVES, if you know what I mean," Octavius replied, clapping Marcus on his very broad back. "You're a completely different class of slave. Gaius would be lost without you, though I can't say I'd entrust the running of MY business to someone of such low birth. An infant warrior of Boudica, no less. You're practically a Barbarian."

"Be that as it may, Mr Octavius, and I say this with respect…" Marcus was interrupted by a yelp from Pip. She was still watching her mum in the field. Carrie had been felled by a blow from the farmhand;

"Can't you do something Marcus, please?" she begged.

"Well, that won't do; it really won't do at all," Octavius said, watching Carrie struggling to get herself from the ground. "Maybe I should send her to the gladiator barracks for some, ahem, more professional training. They have a specific diet, don't you know? Barley and vegetable ash all stewed up with herbs and other muck - 'veganism' I think they call it. It smells like pig swill. Anyway, if I'm going to win my bet, I think that's what I must do."

"I'm heading to the barracks later on to see my friend Cassius. Would you like me to take her in the cart?" Marcus asked, knowing that any slave would be safer at the barracks than with Octavius.

"Cassius?" Octavius asked, "The headline act?"

"Yes sir, he's like a brother to me," Marcus said. "We worked together in the fields when we were boys. If Mr Gaius hadn't picked me for the household, I'd have followed the same path as him. I want to see him before he fights to wish him luck."

"You're a hulk of a man like him, that's for sure, perfect for the arena," Octavius said. "I'm surprised your brain can do battle with all that brawn and come out victor, but yes, that's good of you. I'd be grateful if you could escort her to the barracks. I'll leave her shackled in the dairy. I'll hide the key under the milk bucket. Now let me sort out your order."

Marcus followed Octavius into the farmhouse, leaving Pip with Dentata.

"Did you HEAR that?" Pip said to the mule.

"Indeed, I did. What a horrible man he is." Dentata swished her tail then said, "We can make a run for it on the way to the barracks."

"Yes!" Pip was elated. "I can't wait to meet my mum at last, after all these years."

"Well, you must try and stay calm. We don't want Marcus to suspect anything," Dentata said.

Marcus returned from the house with two slaves belonging to Octavius. He made room in the cart, moving things around while the two men fetched the order from one of the outhouses.

They returned with their arms laden.

"Thanks, mate," Marcus said. "If you could lift it straight onto the cart, that would be great. Make sure you pack the eggs in tight; it will be a bumpy ride back to the house."

"Right, boss," replied the taller of the two men. Pip noticed, dug deeply into his cheek, a deep violet scar that moved with his words.

"Here are all the cabbages, eggs and cheese you ordered. There are a couple of trays of peaches and figs in there and a jar of honey."

"I was stung all over getting that for you," laughed the shorter fellow. He swatted away imaginary bees with his hands. The taller man continued;

"Twelve dormice, already dead, and a cured ham. We'll be back in a second with the olive oil and wine. Just a moment…"

Pip watched the men walk over to where the jars were stored in the ground to keep them cool. They pulled out six large ones and rolled them over to the cart. Marcus helped to lift them up. Dentata's harness shifted with the extra weight.

"Right then," the shorter slave said. "That's all the wine and a jar of our master's finest olive oil. Let me take you to the sty and you can choose your piglets."

Marcus placed his big hands on Pip's shoulders and steered her over the cobbles towards the pigsty. She peered over the door.

Inside, lying on a bed of straw, was a fat sow, snoring loudly while her piglets played. A couple chased each other round the sty.

"Which ones shall we pick, mate?" Marcus asked Pip. "You choose; we're taking three."

"Well," she said, resting her finger on her chin, "I think we should take the spotty one because it's friendly." How lucky Lucius and Tiberia are, she thought, having piglets at home to play with. She wondered if they might stop Tiberia worrying about Dentata; "And we'd better take those two lively ones," she said.

"Well, I don't see how being friendly or lively will make them taste better, but you're right, it's the sign of a healthy animal." Marcus smiled and patted Pip on the shoulder. Pip blanched in horror.

"They will be EATEN?" she exclaimed. "They're just babies."

"That's how the family like them, my boy; young and tender. Yes please…," he addressed the two men, "we'll take those three. The ones my young apprentice picked out, thank you."

"Right you are," the shorter man said, brandishing a shiny blade between his teeth. "Just let us take them into the slaughterhouse. Don't want to make a mess in the yard."

Pip jumped into the cart and covered her ears until the men returned with the dead piglets. He strung them to a pole and attached it to the bottom of the cart so they could be bled on the journey home. Pip edged to the front of the cart, turning her back to them. Her thoughts returned to her mother.

"When will we be coming back for Vesta?" she asked Marcus who had taken up the mule's reins.

"Who?" he said.

"The woman in the field. You know, the gladiator."

"Oh, sometime later on today. We have a few more errands to run first. Why do you ask?"

"Oh, I'd really like to see where the gladiators train," Pip lied. "Can you introduce me to your friend? Was his name Cassius, did you say?"

"Yes, that's right," Marcus said, leading Dentata out of the courtyard. She stumbled onto the road.

"That's a girl, giddy up," he said to encourage her over the stony ground.

"When are the games?" Pip asked.

"Three days before the Ides," Marcus said. Pip was none the wiser.

"When will that be?" she asked.

"Vesta will have just two days left to hone her skills. I don't think it will turn out well for her though, as Crispus is a giant; a one-armed giant but a giant all the same. He took fifty lives over the years before the lion got him and he had to retire. He remains unbeaten. Well, unbeaten by a man. You never know, a woman might do the job, but I don't think that woman is Vesta; she's far too small and incompetent. Being a gladiator is a full-time job. They train for months, years, in fact. Octavius is crazy."

After they'd dropped the food off to a grateful Spurius, Marcus, Pip and Dentata made their way to the fuller's to collect their clean laundry.

"What's a fuller?" Pip asked. She was trying to engage with Marcus even though her mind was on the dairy at Octavius' farm.

"Didn't you have fullers in Greece? I can't believe that. Fulling is a stinky business, mate, worse than making fish sauce." Pip didn't believe him. Nothing could smell worse than fish sauce.

"The fuller launders all our clothes. He also dyes them. That's why we're going today. The family have requested the fanciest colours for their robes to wear at the games. To show how important they are. Master Gaius is funding this year's games so his robes will be lined with purple."

"Like Octavius'?" Pip asked.

"Yes, that man has ideas above his station. I'm amazed Gaius doesn't have a word with him. It's insulting really; he's only a farmer after all. Here we are anyway; jump down."

Pip had seen the fuller's before but today the shutters were closed. She was pleased.

"I don't think it's open, Marcus," she said. "Maybe we should go back to the farm to collect Vesta."

"No, Pip, we have more important things to do today. It might be best if we leave that for tomorrow," Marcus said.

"No!" Pip protested, a little too strongly.

"Look, kid, what is it with you and Vesta? You are obsessed."

"I'm not, Marcus, it's just that Octavius is so cruel, and I can't bear to think of her shackled in a cold dairy. He probably gave her a beating too. Did you see the scar on that slave's face?"

"Yeah, maybe you're right, young Pip. It wouldn't be fair to leave her there for long. She should have a few days away from Octavius, especially considering she's got certain death ahead of her. Actually, I'll have a word with Cassius; see if he can take her under his wing and show her a few moves. Come on, let's get the laundry out of the way. Stephanus' place always looks closed; he's afraid of sunlight."

Marcus heaved the heavy door open. A bell clanged as they went inside. It was gloomy inside the shop. It took a while for Pip's eyes to adjust to the low light.

Marcus had been right about the smell. The laundry smelled like a public convenience. Stephanus appeared behind the counter;

"Good morning, Marcus," he said. "Is it still morning? One can never tell in here."

"Hello, Stephanus sir, we're here for the Ambustus family's posh outfits," Marcus said, "for the games."

"Right you are. And who's this little fellow here? I don't think we've met before."

"This is Pip, our new house-boy. We were just up at Octavius' farm. He's had some crazy idea about the games. You'll never guess what he's done."

"I don't have to guess. It's daubed all over the city," Stephanus laughed. "'Poor woman' is all I can say; Crispus will cut her in two. Although, she DID steal my best bronze bowl. It had belonged to my mother. I can't say that mummy-dearest wouldn't have been upset at my using it as a piddle pot, but bronze is the only metal suitable for the job."

"She certainly seems to have got around. Vesta is her name, Pip said. They were together briefly in the holding pen at the market. Pip said she was kind to him, didn't you, mate?" Marcus touched Pip's shoulder.

"Well then, young Pip, come and help me fetch the clothes for Marcus. Follow me," Stephanus said, lifting the countertop so she could squeeze under.

She followed Stephanus down a long passageway. As they went on, the acrid smell of the shop got stronger. It burned the back of Pip's nose. Stephanus stopped suddenly and drew away a screen barring the entrance to a room. Pip followed him inside.

The room was large and bright. Piles of gleaming white laundry lined the walls, stacked up on shelves. Pip's eyes fell onto the activity at the far end of the room. In four large vats, four weary men were treading on layers of cloth, submerged in urine.

"What are they doing?" Pip asked, pointing at the men.

"My slaves? Why, they're cleaning cloth, boy. The urine acts very well on stubborn stains. See how white they get it?" he said, reaching for Lucius and Tiberia's gleaming tunics from a shelf and handing them to her.

"But what about the slaves' feet?" she asked. "Doesn't it burn?"

"They are prone to blisters, yes," Stephanus said, "but it's best not to dwell on nasty things like that. Just thank the Gods it's not YOUR feet in there."

Pip followed Stephanus back to the dark shop front. She placed the tunics on the counter. Stephanus fetched a step ladder so he could reach the rest of the order.

"I had a bit of trouble with my saffron supplier," he said, reaching up to the top shelf, "but it came just in the nick of time."

"Ah, the yellow-edged stola for Lady Decima," Marcus said. "She'd have played merry Hades if it hadn't been ready in time. I'm sure she's already told her friends how she's going to look like the bee's knees at the games." Marcus took the robe from the fuller.

"And the purple-edged robe for Gaius," Stephanus said. "I'm glad he decided on the edging rather than the full purple. I've always found it a bit too much on Octavius. A bit too grandiose, wouldn't you say?"

"It's not my place to say," Marcus laughed, picking up the family's clothing, "but I think Octavius might put the Emperor in the shade. Thank you, Stephanus. We'll see you at the baths tomorrow."

"I'm looking forward to it," Stephanus said. "Goodbye, Marcus. Goodbye, Pip."

Pip raced to the cart and launched herself over the side.

"Come on, Marcus," she yelled. "Let's hurry to the farm and free Vesta from her shackles."

"Hold your horses, mate," Marcus said, arranging the clothes in the cart so they wouldn't get dirty. "We need to drop these back at the house first."

"But why?" Pip was impatient.

"Because Quinta needs to do some adjustments, THAT'S why. Just calm down. We'll get there eventually."

Pip sat down sulkily in the cart as Dentata staggered forth to get the wheels rolling. The journey seemed to take forever. At last, the cart stopped outside the house.

"Help me bring those in, would you?" Marcus asked.

Pip gathered up the material, jumped from the cart and raced into the house. She shouted a cheerful 'hello' to Quinta who took the clothing from her. Marcus went on into the kitchen.

"How are you finding it here?" Quinta asked Pip.

"Oh, Marcus is nice. We're going to the gladiator barracks now. We're going to take a…" Pip suddenly stopped talking. Marcus emerged from the kitchen followed by Lucius.

"Look who I found," he said. "It seems like you're not the only one desperate to meet Cassius, Pip."

Eleven

"I don't see why you have to bring a slave on a fun outing like this," Lucius said, his face like thunder and his elbows resting on the front of the cart.

"Pip needs to learn, Master Lucius," Marcus said, turning to face the boy as he guided the mule once more to the farm, "He needs to be my shadow for a few years at least. Then, when I am given my freedom, he'll be as useful to you as I am to Master Gaius, your father."

"Don't be silly," Lucius said. "Porcus will never be useful to anybody. Look at him sitting there, rocking on his heels like a simpleton."

Pip was crouching in the back of the cart, trying not to get pigs' blood on her tunic. "He looks about as useful as a girl gladiator. Speaking of which, can I hold on to Malefica in the cart? Just to make sure she doesn't run away? Please, Marcus, can I?" Lucius begged.

"We'll see," Marcus said, "But I won't allow you to be cruel to her. She has enough on her plate as it is. Anyway, the purpose of this trip is to visit Cassius at the barracks. The slave woman should be of no interest to you."

"Cassius is my favourite gladiator EVER," Lucius gushed. "Will you ask him if I can take something of his? Sandals or something. What about a leather wrist guard? Please, Marcus? My friends would be SO jealous. I could have a whole outfit." Lucius jumped out of the cart and vaulted onto Dentata's back to be closer to Marcus. The mule buckled under the extra weight.

"Not today, Lucius. Cassius has other things on his mind, and be careful with Dentata, she's struggling enough to pull the cart as it is," Marcus said.

Lucius grabbed Dentata's mane and jutted his bottom lip out. "What's that stupid ribbon doing in the mule's hair?" he asked, pointing to Dentata's braided forelock. "It looks stupid and girly. I'm going to rip it out," he said, reaching forwards. Marcus slapped away his hand. "You just leave that alone or there'll be trouble. It looks like the work of a very worried and sad little girl. I will personally tan your backside if you touch it."

Dejected, Lucius' thoughts turned back to Carrie.

"Shouldn't criminals be punished?" Lucius asked. "Shouldn't Malefica be made to pay for what she did? She stole from ALL those people. Stealing is bad, Marcus."

"I agree, Lucius, stealing is bad, but the punishment should fit the crime. Vesta, as you should call her, not Malefica, does not deserve to die for stealing."

"But it will be fun to watch her, don't you think?" Lucius said, slicing the air with an imaginary sword. "You like watching your friend Cassius fight, don't you?"

"That's different," Marcus said. "Cassius will be in a fair fight because he is a trained gladiator and he will be fighting another man. His fighting is his life's work and anyway, I wouldn't say I enjoyed watching him as such. I can admire his talent and strength and I am always pleased when he remains uninjured, BUT…"

"I love it when they get cut," Lucius interrupted. "I love to see them fall onto their knees in pain."

Marcus knew his words were wasted and remained silent until they reached the farm.

Lucius jumped off the mule's back before the cart had turned into the farm's courtyard. He began racing round in circles. "Where is she? Where's the thief?" he shouted. Marcus led Dentata to the middle of the yard, then caught the whirling Lucius by the hem of his tunic;

"That's enough, Master Lucius. Go to the house and ask Madam Valentina for a glass of sheep's milk. She'll be pleased to see you."

"But I…" Lucius protested. "No buts," Marcus said firmly, "she's your aunty and would be cross to find out you'd been here and had not been in to see her."

With Lucius safely inside, Pip jumped down from the cart.

"I'll fetch her, shall I?" she offered hopefully. "I can go and get her while you see to Dentata. I think she has a stone in her hoof. She'll be uncomfortable on the trip back if you don't get it out." Pip didn't wait for permission.

"The dairy's next to the slaughterhouse," Marcus shouted after her. "The key is under the milk bucket."

Pip was nervous. She could feel her heart banging against her ribs. She lifted the latch on the dairy door, stepped inside and bolted it behind her. Her mother was huddled in the furthest corner. One of her ankles was shackled to the dairy wall by a thick chain. She was trembling in the cold outhouse, dressed only in rags. Pip approached slowly without saying a word. Carrie raised her eyes. She seemed puzzled.

Pip crouched next to her and took hold of her hand. She warmed it in her own for a few moments then said;

"Mum, it's Pip. Do you recognise me?" She looked into Carrie's eyes, pausing for a moment. "I suppose I've changed a lot in thirteen years. I've come to bring you home." Carrie let out a cry and threw her arms around her.

"My precious baby girl, I have been worried sick," she said, "You're so big. Look at you! I held you in my arms just a few weeks ago, but I must have been gone for so long. I'm so sorry for making you come here. I have put you in danger. It's a terrible place. I didn't know how awful it would be."

"It's okay, it's okay," Pip said quietly, fighting back her own tears. She pulled her mum to her feet and reached to wipe the tears from her face with her thumbs. "We, Dentata and I, that is, were hoping to rescue you today but…"

She was interrupted by a pounding on the door. "Let me in, let me in!" Lucius bellowed.

"As I said, we were hoping to rescue you today, but Lucius came along and spoiled all that. We'll have to think of something else," Pip whispered.

"If you don't let me in now, I'll bash the door down," the boy threatened. Pip could see his forehead above the dairy door.

"I'm just undoing her chains," Pip said. "Hang on, would you?"

"MARCUS!" Lucius yelled. "Porcus is refusing to let me in. Make him, make him at once!"

Pip lifted the milk bucket and found the key.

"He thinks you're a boy," Carrie said, bewildered.

"Mrs Higgins thought it best if I pretended," Pip said. "She thought it would be safer."

She undid the clasp around Carrie's ankle and let it fall to the ground. It had left a red mark. She took her mother's hand and unbolted the door.

Marcus was now standing with Lucius whose face was hot and red.

"The slave didn't obey me," he whined.

"Oh, not now, Lucius," Marcus said. "We need to get to the barracks and back in good time. I have a meeting in town later."

Lucius, Pip and her mum sat on the floor of the cart. Lucius had a ball of string. He wound it around Carrie's wrists.

"Don't think about running away," he said. "I'm holding you fast." Pip and her mum looked at each other. They tried their best to be brave and both gave weak smiles.

The cart rolled back towards town and entered at the Sarno Gate. Marcus took the cart down the Via dell'Abbondanza. They passed the Ambustus house. Lucius stood up, gave a wave and shouted, "We have Malefica, Daddy. We have captured her," even though nobody was home to see him. He sat down again in a huff.

Instead of continuing to the Forum, Marcus turned the cart left up the Stabian Way. They came to a green space behind the theatre.

"Here it is," Marcus said. "These are the barracks." He helped Carrie, whose hands were still bound, jump down from the cart.

Pairs of men were sparring with each other in a small arena enclosed by wooden posts. Several other men, taking a rest, were leaning against the posts. They chatted with each other.

Lucius jumped out of the cart and raced to the edge of the arena.

"Cassius! Cassius!" he called out. The largest of the resting men walked over. He was covered in sweat that made his muscles gleam in the sun. Cassius saw Marcus with the boy.

"Ah, Marcus, my friend. What brings you here? Fancy joining in?" He jabbed his short wooden sword playfully towards his friend. Marcus laughed.

"I've come to wish you luck for the games, of course, and to ask you a favour, mate." Marcus took hold of Carrie's arm and pushed her forward.

"I'm sure you've heard of this woman," he said. "This is Vesta, I believe, though you might know her as Malefica."

"Ah yes," Cassius nodded his head. "Our coach mentioned her. Octavius sent instruction for her to have some intensive training before the games."

"That's right," Marcus said. "The thing is, the odds are stacked against her. Have you heard who she's fighting?"

"Yes," Cassius said. "I believe Crispus is coming out of retirement specially. It's a stupid spectacle if you ask me. What good can come of it?" he looked at Carrie and undid the twine around her wrists.

"Hey! I put that on," Lucius moaned. "Put it back at once." Cassius ignored him.

"Master Lucius is still a spoiled brat, I see," he said, rubbing Carrie's wrists where the string had dug in. Lucius blushed and hid behind Marcus.

"Is there anything you can do with her? Teach her the basics? I know you don't have long."

"I can certainly try. Crispus lost his right arm, didn't he? And I believe he had been right-handed. Let's see if we can come up with some moves to exploit this. Some intelligent footwork might help," Cassius said. "Who's the other fella?" He'd just noticed Pip. "Is this lady your mum?" he asked her.

"No, no, no," Marcus said. "This is Pip. He's our new house-boy." Pip bowed her head.

"Well," Cassius said, "they're like two peas in a pod. Leave it with me and I'll see what I can do."

"Look after her please, Mr Cassius," Pip said.

"I'll do my very best," the big man said, "Hey, Marcus! You know my lucky shield, the one embossed with the gladiator helmet? Someone stole it. Stupidly, I left it outside here overnight. Someone was seen making away with it on the back of a mule. I've asked the blacksmith to make me another one but there might not be enough time. I suppose I'll have to borrow one."

"I wonder who did that," Marcus said. "A pretty low-down thing to do."

"I'm not sure; I've had fans pinch stuff before, but never anything so precious."

"Ah well, don't let it knock your confidence, mate. I believe in you, lucky shield or not. Anyway, gotta dash. See you at the games, and thank you." The two embraced for a short while then Marcus guided Pip and Lucius back to the cart. Pip jumped up then watched Cassius lead her mother into the gladiator dwellings, feeling as if she'd lost her all over again.

Later that day, after she'd eaten dinner, Spurius asked Pip to rub the mule down after her hard day pulling the cart. She let herself in by the side stable door. Grabbing a handful of straw, she rubbed Dentata's sweaty neck using circular strokes.

"Oh… up a bit, that's it, JUST there," the mule said, her withers quivering with pleasure.

"I've been thinking," said Pip, "we need to return the shield to Cassius. It's his lucky shield. I'd feel dreadful if he lost his fight because he was superstitious about not having it."

He IS being good to Carrie," agreed Dentata, "but returning to the barracks would be foolish. It's a big old thing; you'd be seen carrying it."

"What if we framed Lucius? What if we hid it in his room to make it look as if he'd stolen it?"

"Isn't that a bit risky?" Dentata swished her tail.

"I've made up my mind," Pip was resolute, "I'm going to do it; tonight. I can hear Spurius calling me. Gotta dash," was all she said before quickly leaving the stable and bolting the door.

Later on, after dark, Pip waited until all the men in the slaves' quarters were snoring soundly. She trod lightly down the stairs, tiptoed through the hall and gently parted the green curtain that led to the garden. A big round moon lit her way to the stable, and gently, she lifted the door latch.

"Well, you rushed off pretty quickly earlier. Is it safe for you to be here? What if someone misses you?"

"I'm sorry. I didn't want you to change my mind and the men won't notice me gone. They're fast asleep and snoring." She knelt in the straw and felt for the shield. She grabbed it with both hands and heaved it up.

"Wow," she said. "It weighs a tonne."

"Just you be careful," the mule advised. "If you get caught with it, that'll be the end of everything."

"I know," Pip said. She bade Dentata goodnight and left the stable.

Pip put her arm through the strap at the back of the shield. It was easier to carry it that way. She goofed around in the moonlight, imagining she was in the amphitheatre. She moved back and forth, waving her free arm in the air. Startled by a rustling in the laurels, she ducked behind the Bacchus statue. It was only the peacock.

Pip emerged from the statue and tiptoed carefully back through the garden and hauled the shield through the curtain. She waited outside the children's room. She put the shield down and listened. She could hear two distinct snoring sounds through the screens; Lucius' thin and rasping, Tiberia making an occasional snort. She picked up the shield and squeezed past the screens.

Lucius was sleeping in the bed nearest the window. Unlike Tiberia, who slept on a mattress like Pip's, Lucius had a bed with a proper wooden frame and a mattress filled with wool. The room was bright with moonlight. Pip crept over and bent down next to the bed. Lucius was lying on his back. Pip could smell his breath. It was hot and sour.

He stirred momentarily and turned to face the wall. Pip took her chance. She grabbed the shield, placing it flat on the floor, shiny side up. She gently slid it under Lucius' bed. Lucius stirred again and turned back to face her, making the bed creak. Pip held her breath.

Lucius resumed his snoring and Pip gently exhaled with relief. She gave the shield a final shove, making sure it was well hidden. She then picked up one of the boy's sandals and tiptoed back to the screens, taking care not to kick any of the toys lying around on the floor. She was rather pleased with herself but hadn't noticed Tiberia watching her from her mattress on the floor. Pip closed the screens, hid the sandal on a shelf in the kitchen, skimmed up the stairs and slid under her thin grey blanket.

Twelve

The following morning, Pip was in the kitchen helping Spurius with the workers' lunches. She was planning Lucius' downfall. When would be the best time to 'find' Cassius' shield? She thought she might stub her toe on it when collecting the children's chamber pots early next morning. Yes, that would be an excellent time to do it.

She'd just made up her mind when she heard shouting coming from the corridor. Spurius groaned, flipped his tea towel over his shoulder and left the kitchen to investigate. Pip followed him.

"What's all this nonsense? If you're not careful, you'll wake your mother. She's exhausted after her trip." Spurius slid aside the screens outside the children's bedroom, "Well I never! What have you got there?"

Pip squeezed around the fat cook and was surprised to see Tiberia sitting cross-legged on her mattress, holding the huge shield unsteadily on her knees.

"Tiberia, where on earth did you get that thing? That doesn't belong to you."

"Lucius took it from the gladiators' barracks," she said calmly. "He stole it."

All eyes fell upon the boy who swung his feet over the side of his bed to sit up. He rubbed his eyes.

"I didn't do it. I didn't."

"I found it under his bed. I shouted for help immediately." Tiberia went on, "He'd tried to cover it with a dirty tunic."

Lucius stood up and approached Tiberia. He fell onto his knees and reached out to touch the cool metal of the engraving on the shield.

"Cassius…" he whispered.

"Stealing is wrong," Tiberia shouted. "I'm telling Daddy."

"What's the commotion? The sun's not even up yet!" Marcus appeared at the doorway. "Well, blow me down. Is that Cassius' shield?" He pushed his way into the room.

"Lucius stole it," Tiberia declared, "and I found it under his bed."

"How could you do such a thing?" Marcus bent down and took the shield from Tiberia, "This is so precious to Cassius. How could you?"

"But I didn't… I…"

"You took the mule in the night, didn't you? You said you wanted to take something of his. You actually took the mule and rode to the barracks and took my friend's shield. What a low down, rotten thing to do. How could you?"

"I didn't take it. I swear on Bacchus, Marcus."

"How did it get under your bed then?"

Lucius started to cry.

"I'm not interested in tears. You really have over-stepped the mark. You can stay in here until I've decided what to do with you." Marcus raised the shield over his arm, barged past Spurius and Pip and left the room.

Lucius rubbed his eyes. Slowly he looked up and saw Pip. She was standing with her arms folded, a tiny smile starting at the corners of her lips.

"You," Lucius hissed, "you did this."

"I don't know what you're talking about," Pip said.

"It's always best to own up," said Spurius, hauling Lucius to his feet, "then you can say sorry and try to mend things. I suggest you have a little think on your own about what you've done. Maybe hunger will help you to reflect. Tiberia, you come with us. Pip will make you some breakfast."

Spurius guided the boy back to his bed and told him to sit down. "You stay here until Marcus says so." He ushered the girls out of the bedroom and closed the screens firmly.

Tiberia took a chunk of bread from Pip and sat on the latrine to eat it.

"Don't eat there, there are too many germs. Come and sit on this stool; it's cleaner." Tiberia ignored her, wiping crumbs from her hands onto her tunic.

"I saw you put the shield under Lucius' bed in the night. I was awake. I had one eye open and I saw you."

"Well," Pip said, "why didn't you snitch? You could have done. You could have told Marcus."

"Because I don't like Lucius. He's mean to me. And I like you. You are kind. He wouldn't shut up last night about Cassius and how he'd had his shield stolen and how he wished he could find it and keep it for himself. He said someone rode to the barracks in the night, took it and rode away on a mule. He seemed quite happy about it." Tiberia looked sad.

"Lucius says I'm only a girl and girls are rubbish and they smell and when I grow up, I'll only be a woman and he'll be a man and men are the best. Sometimes he pinches me really hard. Did you steal the shield from Cassius?"

"No, Tiberia, I didn't. I was cleaning out Dentata's stable yesterday and I found it buried in the straw. I found this with it."

Pip bent down to pick something from a low shelf. She stood up and handed it to Tiberia. It was Lucius' sandal.

"Why didn't you tell straight away? Why did you hide it under his bed?"

"Oh, come on, Tiberia. Who would have believed me? I'm a slave boy don't forget, and Lucius is the son of a senator. I would probably have been whipped for my troubles, or cast out, or worse…"

"Mummy believes everything he says," Tiberia paused to take a bite of the bread, "but he's in big trouble now."

The girls were interrupted by Marcus. He banged his head on the pots and pans as he entered the kitchen.

"Come on you two, we're going to give Cassius his shield back."

"Just us two? Is Lucius not coming?" Tiberia was beside herself with glee.

"Certainly not. He's staying in his room for the time being. Until

Hades gets cold, if I have my way. Meet me at the front. The cart is ready. I'll just fetch the mule."

Tiberia sat close to Pip on the journey to the gladiators' barracks.

"I can't believe Marcus is taking me and not Lucius," she said, over and over again.

The cart rolled to a halt and Tiberia jumped out, raced around to Dentata and gave her a rub under her braided forelock. The mule whinnied and nuzzled the little girl.

"Come on, Tiberia, there's no time for that." Marcus reached into the cart and lifted out the shield as if it was made of feathers. "Follow me."

Marcus strode to the edge of the empty practice area. He placed the shield behind the two girls telling them to make sure it was hidden and gave a piercing whistle. Nothing happened. He cupped his hands to his mouth and bellowed, "CASSIUS!"

After a few moments, a small boy appeared.

"Can I help you, sir?"

"I've come to see Cassius. Is he here?"

"The gladiators are having their morning massage. Is it important?"

"Oh, have I missed him? Are they at the baths?"

"No sir, the Stabian Baths are closed so the masseur came to the barracks."

"Great. Can you fetch him then, please? Tell him his friend Marcus is here and I have something for him."

"Well, I can ask him, but I can't promise anything; you know what they're like." The boy bounded away and disappeared into the barracks.

A few minutes later, Cassius emerged from the building. He waved and crossed the grass. He looked sleepy and his body glistened with olive oil.

"You need the strigil," Marcus said laughing. "You're dripping."

"I came quickly. What's happened? Is everything alright?"

"Yes, my friend. Everything is peachy."

"Oh, come on, mate, did you disturb my routine to tell me everything is peachy? I'm fighting, possibly to the death I might add, in a few days' time." His face softened when he noticed the two girls,

"Look, I'm sorry for being snappy. You know I get a bit twitchy before a fight."

"It's ok, mate, I understand. I think you might be glad of the interruption though. Pip, show Cassius what we've got for him."

Pip turned around and bent to pick up the shield. She heaved it up from the floor and gave it to Marcus.

"You found it!" Cassius vaulted the fence, grasped his shield from his friend, lifted it into the air and kissed it. "Where was it? Where did you find it? I am SO pleased. Thank you SO much!" He put his arm through the leather straps and held it in front of his chest. "Boy, have I missed this. It fits me like a glove. Who took it? Let me know so I can hammer them into next week. Though I don't suppose it really matters now that I have it back."

"Well, it's a bit embarrassing really," Marcus shifted his feet uneasily and looked at the floor. "Remember you said someone was seen leaving with it on the back of a mule? In the night?"

"Yes…"

"Well…"

"Go on, spit it out."

"It was Master Lucius."

Cassius burst out laughing. "What a little turd! Master Lucius is spoiled enough. Why would he start stealing? I'm sure Gaius would have had one made up for him specially if he'd only asked."

"For the thrill of it maybe. Who knows what goes on in that kid's head? Anyway, you have Tiberia to thank for its safe return. She found it hidden under his bed and told me straight away.

"Well, thank you, Miss," Cassius bent low and ruffled Tiberia's hair. "Thank you so much. When I win my fight, it will all be thanks to you. Now, give me a minute and I'll see what I can find to give you as a way of saying thank you. I'll send the boy out with something."

"Before you go, Cassius," Pip stepped forward, "how is Vesta? You know, Malefica?"

"Not now, Pip; Cassius is a busy man."

"No, it's ok, I was actually going to mention her. We've not had her for long clearly, but we did a session with her yesterday. She's quite nifty on her feet. What she lacks in strength, she might make up for with technique. You never know… maybe I'll let her use my lucky shield."

Tiberia wore the gladiator helmet all the way home. Even though it had been made for a young boy, it was far too big for her and sat low, resting on her collar bones.

"Lucius will be so cross when he sees this. You won't let him take it from me, will you, Marcus?" Her voice had a metallic echo.

"If he lays so much as a finger on it, I'll tan his hide," Marcus shouted over his shoulder. "Actually, I think it's about time you had your own room. Maybe we can convert Fortuna's office into a bedroom. She's not at the house much and she's leaving us soon. I'm sure she wouldn't mind."

As soon as they reached home, Tiberia took off her helmet, jumped down from the cart and raced towards the house.

"Spurius, Spurius, look what I've got," she yelled as she disappeared inside.

"I'll put the mule away. Can you go into the children's room and gather up Tiberia's things please, Pip?" She jumped down while Marcus unhitched the cart and led Dentata to the back of the house.

Pip cleared her throat loudly and slowly withdrew the screens outside the children's bedroom.

"What do YOU want?" Lucius was sitting on the edge of his bed.

"I've come to collect Tiberia's things, Master Lucius."

"Why?"

"She's moving into the office."

"Says who?"

"Marcus said so, Master Lucius." Pip bent down and began to roll Tiberia's mattress up. Lucius jumped up and stamped his foot down hard on Pip's hand.

"Ouch, that hurt." Pip recoiled and looked at the back of her hand. It had started to redden.

"Nobody asked ME about Tiberia moving out," he shouted, puffing his chest out, arms akimbo.

"Well, that's none of my business, Master Lucius, and if you'll just let me get on with what I've been asked to do…"

Tiberia then barged into the room.

"Look what I've got." She held the helmet high above her head. "Look what Cassius gave me." She walked up to her brother and held it up to his face. Lucius snatched the helmet from her and turned away from her, holding it into his chest.

"You're not to have it. Marcus said. Give it back."

Spurius appeared at the doorway.

"Give the helmet to Tiberia," he sighed. "Give the helmet back and go and sit on your bed. Tiberia, Pip, fetch your things and follow me."

Spurius drew the bedroom screens shut and proceeded down the hall followed by the girls whose arms were full of Tiberia's belongings. He gave a brisk knock on the office screens and paused.

"Enter." Fortuna was sitting at a desk which was littered with papyrus scrolls. She was peering at the wax tablet she was holding. The cook peeked around the door.

"Yes, Spurius, what can I do for you? I'm rather busy." Spurius seemed nervous;

"I'm sorry to bother you, Fortuna, but Marcus asked me to move Tiberia's things into the office. I hope you don't mind."

"It's rather inconvenient. I have a lot of work to do. What's wrong with the children's bedroom?"

"It's Lucius. He's bullying his little sister something shocking. Marcus thought it was time she had her own space."

"I see; in that case, I can make a little room, as long as she's quiet. Fetch her things in and I'll finish what I'm doing. I have a meeting in town with one of Gaius' suppliers."

"Thank you, Fortuna." Spurius turned back into the corridor, relieved. "Tiberia, you go and play in the garden. Pip, can you take her things in then come and help me in the kitchen?"

Pip, holding the mattress, squeezed into the room. She was startled by Fortuna's voice. It was direct but a little husky.

"Ah, I was wondering when we'd meet. I've been expecting you. Draw the screens behind you."

Pip dropped the mattress and did as she was told.

"Come closer; I won't bite."

Pip approached the desk. Fortuna was slim and elegant. Her hair was braided and tied with a bronze clasp at her nape. She wore a white stola, trimmed with green.

"So," she said, looking directly into Pip's eyes, "you're the girl who's come to rescue her mother."

Thirteen

"What makes you think I'm a girl?" Pip was miffed at having her cover blown.

"I just had to look at you; besides, I was expecting a girl. Pull up that stool; we don't have long. You did the right thing though, pretending to be a boy. Pompeii is a very dangerous place for girls, especially slave girls. I was one myself, so I speak from experience."

"Yes, Spurius told me you used to belong to the Faustus family. I think he's scared of you."

"Good. It helps with the image."

"He told me you practice magic and study animal guts. Is it true?"

"Sort of." Fortuna shifted in her seat. "Are those screens closed properly? I don't want anyone to hear this."

Pip dipped into the hall and peered around.

"There's nobody there."

"Okay, it's a long story but I'll be quick. I started Roman life as a household slave, much like you, but the female version. One day, I was about your age. What are you? Thirteen?" Pip nodded. "Yes, I thought so, anyway, we were preparing a bull's carcass for a family feast. I was chopping up the offal for the dogs' dinners and noticed something strange about the liver. It had a peculiar growth in it."

"Ew! Yuk…"

"Yes, have you ever smelled fresh liver? Not pleasant at all but I soon got over it. Well, actually, I'm a vegetarian now but I digress."

"What happened then?" Pip was keen to hear the story.

"Just as I was telling the chief cook all about it, the strange liver that is, the master of the house happened to come into the kitchen looking for a snack and he heard me talking. My hands were dripping with blood and I was excitedly chatting away. I must have seemed quite mad.

He listened for a while without me noticing him. I was gabbling on about the bull, saying that had he not been slaughtered, his days would have been numbered anyway due to the growth, then he interrupted me and told me to bring the liver to his room. I did as I was told. He asked me to look at the liver again and say what I saw.

By this point, I realised I might have accidentally increased my worth as a slave. I started to say I saw things that weren't there. You know, visions of doom and gloom and general unpleasantness.

It just so happened that my master was about to sign a very important business deal, one that could have either doubled his fortune or sent him to the gutter. He immediately pulled out of the deal, and, luckily for me, the man he was about to go into business with was arrested for fraud."

"Wow," Pip said. "That was lucky."

"Yes, so from then on, I became the family's soothsayer if you like, but I got smart with it. Sometimes I became catatonic and wouldn't perform unless I was given coins. This went on for years and I amassed a considerable amount of money. Then there came a time when I had enough money to buy my freedom."

"Did you see my story in a bull's liver?" Pip asked, "Is that how you know who I am?"

"No, don't be silly. It's all complete guff. I met your mother at the slave auction. Every week, I take food and drink to the slaves because the slave trader is an evil devil. They are always hungry and thirsty. He lets me do it in case I put a spell on him.

I have seen the adverts for her fight anyway; what a ludicrous spectacle. I remember Crispus, her opponent. He's a beast of a man."

"You spoke to my mum? What did she say?"

"She told me she'd been arrested for stealing from the Satri family and that she hoped you, her daughter, 'Pip', would come along and save her. She said you'd know where to find her. She was frantic with worry. I said I'd look out for you. And here we are.

You need to get a move on, though, if you're going to rescue her. The volcano is about to blow. You know, that sleepy-looking hummock covered in trees? That's Vesuvius. It's been dormant for many years but it's about to wake up and quite violently, I suspect."

"What?"

Pip's mouth fell open. How did Fortuna know? Had her mum said something?

"I've tried to warn people, but nobody is interested. All they care about is their wealth and their fine houses. There was a huge earthquake here, ooh, fifteen years or so ago. It ruined a lot of the city's plumbing and destroyed a few buildings. The good people of Pompeii think their Gods have had their fun and that's the end of it. They walk around like sheep. They don't think it's ominous that the water is drying up and earth tremors are becoming more frequent."

"I see…"

"Which brings me to your predicament."

"What will you do when… you know… when the thing happens…?"

"Oh, I'll be gone by then, I hope. I'm leaving on the day of the games. I'm working on the Pompeii annual games accounts with Gaius. Once it's all done and dusted, I'll collect my fee and I'll be off. I've purchased rather a nice villa for myself in Misenum; near enough to travel there by foot but far enough away to escape the blast. I've done the maths.

When you rescue your mother, come and find me and I will hide you. Misenum is across the bay of Naples. My villa is on the Via Rosea Domum. You'll know it when you see it. It's the pink house.

Now look, I have to go into town. Meet me here tomorrow at noon. I have a plan to help you. I'll say I'm sending you on an errand. They won't argue."

Fortuna rose from behind the desk, gathered up her stola and swished out of Tiberia's new bedroom.

After lunch that day, Marcus walked with Pip to the Forum Baths. They stopped outside to wait for Gaius.

"What's that building opposite?" Pip asked.

"That's the Temple of Fortuna." Pip smiled and thought of her new friend with the same name. She was pleased to have her help and wondered what her plan was.

The sun shone high in a clear blue sky. It felt good on Pip's skin while they waited for the master of the house. Pip was a bit nervous. She'd only met Gaius briefly at the slave auction. She didn't really know what to expect.

He seemed to creep up behind them;

"Good morning, boys. What a super day. Are the others here yet? Have they already gone in?"

"Not yet, sir," Marcus turned around, "though you must know by now, those two aren't known for being punctual."

"Oh, I DO wish they'd get a move on. I'm a very busy man. My leisure time is precious."

Pip was pleased the farmer was coming. He might have news about her mum.

"Well, sir, I hope you'll be able to hear yourselves talking over the racket in there. It's terribly busy with the Stabian AND the Central Baths being closed. Ah, here they come now."

Two crumpled shapes emerged in the distance, one tall, one very short. Neither seemed to be in much of a hurry. They approached Gaius half-heartedly.

"Ah, Octavius, my friend," Gaius said, clapping him enthusiastically on the back. Octavius grimaced.

"Oh, too much wine last night, eh? Never mind, you can sweat it out in the baths." He turned to Stephanus.

"Stephanus, my dear man. How is life in the laundry? Are things going well?"

"Yes, Gaius, I've struggled a bit with the water supply of late, but as long as people keep spilling wine on their togas and egg yolk on their tunics, I'm in business."

"Ah, that's good. Now come on, chaps, let's get in, shall we?"

Gaius swept his friends through the entrance of the baths. Pip and Marcus followed behind.

"Don't worry, my dear fellows, this is on me. I want us all to have a nice relaxing time. I've been tearing my hair out with all the preparations for the games. It will be good to switch off for an hour." He took out some coins to pay the entrance fee. The attendant recognised him and told him to put his money away.

"There's no need for that, Senator Gaius. Just go on in. You might find it gets a bit cramped, mind. I can only apologise. If you're quick, you might be able to nab a good spot."

Gaius turned to Octavius.

"You came without a slave, I see. I like to have Marcus beside me when I can; he's such a help and he's training up our new house boy."

"Yes, I met the boy at my farm. He seemed to be rather interested in my new acquisition. You know… the cat burglar."

"Do you really think that's such a good idea?" Gaius asked, ushering his friends into the changing room. "It will be over pretty quickly if you ask me. One stroke of Crispus' sword, in fact." Pip blanched. She tried to distract herself by looking around the building. The changing rooms were elaborately decorated with plaster mouldings set against bright yellow walls. The mouldings were painted and showed scenes of men reclining in the baths. Octavius went on;

"Nonsense, nonsense… she's a firebrand that one. I think she'll put up a heck of a fight. If it ends badly for her, at least we'll have been entertained. She'll draw a huge crowd for you. Have you not heard the chatter about town? You should be grateful to me for that at least."

"Well, yes, there is that, but I don't want my games to be remembered for the wrong reasons, Octavius."

As the group started to undress, more men entered the changing rooms. It became noisy and crowded. Pip hid behind Marcus. Gaius shouted over to him as he flung his toga into a wooden locker.

"Are you not joining in, Marcus? You're still in your clothes."

Marcus turned and looked at Pip. She became pale and stepped away from him. Could she make a run for it? She could not be made to undress.

"Not today, sir, I'm looking after the boy." Pip exhaled.

"Ah, that's a pity. You've been working hard all week."

"They're supposed to work hard. They are slaves, Gaius," Octavius piped up. He was lingering by the lockers with Stephanus. They were taking far too much time folding their clothes.

"Be that as it may, my dear man, Marcus here deserves a little pampering every now and then. Anyway, hurry up now, chaps." Gaius was becoming impatient. "Let's get out of here. We need to get comfortable before the place fills up. Tell you what, I'll head straight for the hot room. Let's bypass the preliminaries, shall we? See you in five." He squeezed his way through a group of young men who had just arrived laughing and shouting, and flounced out of the changing rooms.

"Come on, Pip," Marcus said, "I need to stay by his side."

Gaius charged into the warm room, sped through and disappeared out of the other side. Marcus strode after him. Pip paused to look around. The room was magnificent with its rows of statues lining the bath, which was, sadly, as dry as a bone. Three impressive statues of muscular men seemed to be holding up the ceiling. She loved seeing Pompeii in real life. It was so much better than looking at pictures in a book.

Her reverie was shattered by a whistle.

"What are you doing?" Marcus shouted. He had turned back to find her. Pip rushed out of the warm room to join him. Marcus hissed at her;

"There's no time to be dilly-dallying, Pip. We are here to look after Master Gaius. This isn't about YOU."

"I'm sorry, Marcus, I've never been to the baths before and I just…"

"Never mind that now; follow me."

Marcus led Pip down a narrow corridor. She could feel the floor getting warm under her feet.

"Ah, Master Gaius, already enjoying the steam, I see." Marcus and Pip entered the hot room. Gaius' face was already red. He was sitting on a wooden bench, sweating profusely. He seemed upset.

"Two louts barged in, Marcus, Ajax and his brother," he said, "Have you met them? Rather uncouth they are but I told them this room was taken. They weren't best pleased and will probably come back to try their luck. Where ARE the other two?"

Octavius and Stephanus shuffled in. "Speak of the devils. Come in, my good fellows. The steam is excellent."

The two dilatory men joined Gaius on the bench. Marcus and Pip withdrew to rest against the back wall.

"I don't like the hot room," Octavius complained. "It's far too… well, frankly, it's far too hot."

Gaius leaned over and clapped his friend on the back.

"Nonsense, my dear chap. Can't you feel all stress and strains of the week rising to the surface and evaporating through your pores?"

"Well, not exactly, no."

"Just relax, my good man, and let the heat do its thing. This is JUST what I need after a busy week; quality time relaxing with my friends. No women to spoil our fun. Time out for the boys."

"The only beast more worthless than a woman is a slave," Octavius said, craning his neck to find Marcus with his narrowing eyes. "I really don't know why you insisted on bringing him." Gaius ignored him.

"Let's discuss the games, shall we? I must say I was absolutely thrilled to be elected Senator last year. Being able to put on the annual games for the good people of Pompeii is the stuff of dreams; my dreams anyway."

"Yes, it's amazing what money can buy these days. That fish sauce of yours appears to move mountains as well as the population's bowels, fetid gloop that it is."

Gaius laughed a little too loudly and falsely.

"Now, now, my friend, don't be like that. You and your good lady wife will be joining us RIGHT at the front, ring-side seats no less. How is Valentina keeping? Is she well? I'm looking forward to seeing her tomorrow at my dinner party."

"She keeps herself busy spending all my money," Octavius said closing his eyes, hoping that Gaius would stop talking. "Stephanus is a very lucky man not having a wife to support. They bleed a man dry."

Stephanus looked pained, his sharp bones digging into the hard wooden bench. He fidgeted trying to get comfortable. Sweat ran down his wrinkled face. Gaius jumped up suddenly, letting his towel drop to the floor. He padded over to the hot pool and lowered himself in;

"Ooh, cripes, it's boiling. Come and join me, Stephanus. It will work wonders for your arthritis."

"Yes, I think I'll give it a go. Gosh, you're right." Stephanus took a sharp intake of breath as he lowered his tiny frame into the water. "I think we might cook in here."

"If you two simmering hams wouldn't mind cooking quietly, I would like to have a doze." Octavius closed his eyes and apart from the occasional 'ooh ahh' coming from Gaius as he bobbed in the blistering water, the room fell silent for a few minutes.

A man appeared at the doorway.

"Excuse me, Senator Gaius." Octavius snapped open his eyelids and tutted loudly at the intrusion. Gaius beamed from his hot bath, thrilled at having been recognised.

"Citizen of Pompeii, come and join me; the water's lovely. How can I help? Tell me your name."

"I won't bathe for now, thank you. I'm here with friends. My name is Cornelius, sir. I am a taxpaying citizen and have a matter of the…"

"Are you looking forward to the games, Cornelius? I promise you, the games will be the most spectacular the good people of Pompeii will ever have witnessed."

"I don't give two hoots about the games. What I DO care about is our water supply. What is going on?"

"Well, now, here's the thing," Gaius offered, wringing his hands meekly. "That IS a bit of a problem, I agree, but it's in the hands of the Gods, I'm afraid. The wells have dried up. I can't see what I…"

"I suppose it's the fault of the Gods that rubbish is piling up in the streets and repairs from sixteen years ago are yet to be made," Cornelius interrupted.

Gaius levered himself out of the hot pool. His whole body was crimson. Just as he was placing a soothing arm around Cornelius' shoulders, two burly men appeared at the doorway. Cornelius stepped away from Gaius.

"Here are my friends now. Senator Gaius, can I introduce you to Ajax and his brother Justus?"

Octavius was very annoyed at having his peace disturbed.

"Can't you see we're trying to relax, dammit? Take yourselves out of this hot room and find someone else to harass. For the sake of Bacchus, leave us alone!"

Ajax, the tallest of the three men, recognised Octavius;

"I know you. You were in the bar last night, roaring drunk. I'm amazed you're still alive, the amount of wine you managed to sink. This man, this friend of yours, Senator Gaius, insulted my wife. He said she was a donkey."

"Because she brays like one. In fact, I am sure I saw her pull a cartload of bricks through town this morning," Octavius said, closing his eyes again.

"Now, now, gentlemen, let us not descend into vulgarity." Gaius picked up his towel and wrapped it around his waist.

"I will not have that inebriate malign my household. I'll wipe that smug smile from your face, you…" Ajax strode over to Octavius who was grinning widely without bothering to open his eyes. His eyes were quick to open, however, when Ajax put his hands around his throat and lifted him into the air. Gaius started to panic.

"Marcus, please, do something!"

Marcus stepped out of the shadows and placed a hand on Ajax's shoulder.

"Let him go," he said, calmly.

"I will not. I will hug his neck until all the life leaves him." Octavius' face had turned purple with engorged blood. Marcus, the taller of the men by at least a foot, took Ajax back and wrapped his arm around his neck. He started to squeeze.

"Leave off him!" Cornelius shouted from the doorway. "Justus, let's get him!"

Marcus' grip had sent Ajax to sleep, leaving Octavius to slump back onto the bench. He let Ajax slide gently to the floor and turned around. Slipping to avoid a jab from Cornelius, he shot a straight right into his chin. There were now two men in a heap on the floor. Justus, realising that Marcus was a formidable adversary, held his hands up;

"Don't hit me, please. It's okay. I will take them home. I'm sorry, Senator, for ruining your bath time."

The two floored men started to come to their senses.

"Help them up, Marcus," Gaius said, "there's a good sport."

Marcus and Justus hauled the injured men to their feet and helped them out of the hot room and into the corridor.

"Make sure you help them out onto the street," Gaius shouted after them. He turned to Octavius who was rubbing his neck. "You see now why I like to have Marcus with me at times like these? The man was sent to me by the Gods."

"You're going to be stuck in ten years' time, aren't you? You have promised him his freedom after all."

"I did promise, yes. But a promise can be taken back, my good man. I can easily change the goalposts. Ten years, fifteen years, twenty years. I will keep Marcus forever and he won't find out until it's too late."

"What about the boy you bought to replace him?"

"Ah, well, I dare say he'll be pressing fish guts in the factory before long."

Pip stayed silent, her back against the wall. Marcus would find out he was to be enslaved forever and she would be the one to tell him.

Fourteen

"Marcus, I need to speak to you." Pip rushed into the hallway, trying to catch him before he left the house.

"Not now, Pip. I'm late." Marcus strode over the dog mosaic by the door.

"But I heard Gaius… at the baths yesterday… while you were gone."

"Please, Pip, not now. I am very, very busy. Get on with your work." He turned to face her, irritated, "Gaius and Decima have their dinner party tonight and Fortuna asked for you to be excused at lunchtime; the Gods know how we can do without you at a time like this but what Fortuna wants, Fortuna usually gets. Run along now, will you?"

Dejected, Pip resumed her daily chores. The house was still quiet. She collected all the chamber pots, taking great care not to wake Madam Decima who had returned from her trip to Naples. Her room smelled of heavy, musky perfume. All she could see of her mistress was a mound of auburn hair, lying like a sleeping cat on her pillow. She risked a prolonged peek at the jewels splashed all over her dressing table before hurrying away.

She sloshed out all the pots into the latrine and gave them a rinse. Spurius' big red face appeared, dodging the pots and pans as he entered the tiny kitchen.

"Ah, good morning, Pip; up with the lark again, I see." He yawned and rubbed his eyes. "Those thin mattresses play havoc with my back," he said, placing his fists at the bottom of his spine and leaning backwards. How I long for a feather one, just like Madam Decima's. They don't know how lucky they are, these people."

"I heard Gaius say something bad yesterday."

Spurius started to laugh.

"Welcome to Pompeii, son."

"No really; it was about Marcus."

Spurius became stern. "A slave is to be seen and not heard, my dear boy." He bent down so his eyes were level with Pip's. "Especially a little slave boy like yourself. Now, run along and fetch me the vegetables from the shed. I have a lot of work to do today. Oh, Fortuna asked to borrow you at noon. Bacchus only knows what she has in store for you. Maybe she sensed 'the gift' in you. Or perhaps she wants you to rummage through some entrails. Fancy that?"

"Um, not really."

"Well, don't be late for her or she'll turn you into a frog."

Pip kept an eye on the sundial all morning and at midday, knocked on Tiberia's new bedroom screens.

"Hello; come and sit down." Fortuna was sitting at her desk. She crossed her long legs and leant back in her chair, making a lattice with her fingers.

"Here is my plan. We need to drug Crispus before his fight with your mother."

"What with?"

"Hemlock."

"Do you have some? How will we get him to take it?"

"I don't have any, no, but you will have some by this afternoon."

"Where will I get it from? A chemist's shop?"

"No, you will pick it yourself. There's a small pool next to an olive grove up past Octavius' farm."

"Oh yes, I know it."

"Good. Hemlock plants grow in the moist soil there. Take the mule; it's quite a distance,"

"What do they look like?"

"They are quite tall plants, about your chest height. They have small white flowers in the summer, each having five petals. Most will have blown off by now, but you'll know hemlock best by the purple blotches on its green stalks."

"Do I pull some up from the roots?"

"No. Bring back six leaves. Six to eight leaves is a fatal dose. We don't want to kill him, just send him to sleep but he's a big man and the plant isn't so toxic in autumn."

"Then what should I do?"

"Grind the leaves up with a dash of olive oil, with a pestle and mortar. Make sure that you don't get any on your fingers and wash your hands thoroughly afterwards. Then you must throw the pestle and mortar away. You'll need to put it into Crispus' drink an hour or so before his fight."

"How will I do that?"

"That, my dear, is up to you. Good luck. And don't forget, mine is the pink house in Misenum. I will be expecting you." Fortuna rose from behind the desk, gathered up her stola and glided through the screens.

"I'm off to run that errand for Fortuna," Pip shouted into the kitchen. She didn't wait for a response but hurried over the garden into Dentata's stable. She found the mule ripping her old potato sack tunic into shreds with her teeth.

"What are you doing?" Pip clattered through the stable door.

"Well, it may have escaped your attention that there are no plastic bags here. Nothing of the sort. When you pick the hemlock leaves, you can fold them up in this material and I will keep them safe between my lip and my gums." Dentata curled back her top lip to reveal an expanse of flesh the colour of candy floss.

"Gosh," said Pip, "We could have hidden Cassius' shield in there!"

"Don't be so impertinent." Dentata playfully swished her tail, catching Pip's shoulder.

"I'd better put your bridle on, to show we mean business." Pip fastened the leather strap under the mule's chin then hopped onto her friend's back. She had to bend low as they left the stable street-side.

"The weather is so lovely here," said Pip, letting the reins fall onto Dentata's neck. "Much nicer than back home. I used to freeze half to death in that murky canal. Then, when I got home, Toothless was always hogging the fire. But here, the sun warms my skin, and everything has a brightness to it. Don't you think?"

116

"I miss England actually. I miss the seasons and I miss the rain. Have you ever carried a load of bricks in the scorching sun? I dare say you haven't."

"Well, no, but nobody should be made to do that, not even a mule."

"Quite."

The mule picked up her pace and trotted the length of the Via dell'Abbondanza. The friends left the town walls and passed the mausoleum statues. When they reached the stony ground, Dentata progressed to a wobbly canter. Pip squeezed her legs around the mule's fat tummy to stop herself from falling off.

"Scream if you want to go faster!" the mule whinnied, mimicking a dodgem car operator as she sped through Octavius' fields, kicking up dirt in her wake. Pip clung on for dear life.

Snorting, Dentata came to an abrupt halt at the pool. "I suppose you didn't think a mule could gallop," she panted. She shook her neck and trembled, splashing globes of sweat onto Pip, "Boy, that felt good. I've not done that for years."

Pip slid off her back onto trembling legs. "Maybe we could enter you for the Grand National when we get home."

"My dear girl, I might take a look at the spectacle from the stands, but I hope to be very much a human by then. Anyway, chop-chop, go and pick some hemlock." Dentata stooped to tear up some lush green grass with her enormous yellow teeth.

"Bon appetite," Pip called out and disappeared into the foliage.

She returned a few minutes later, carefully holding the leaves in a piece of cloth. "I took care not to touch them with my fingers. I picked twelve, you know, just in case."

"Are you sure you picked the right ones?"

"Yes, I think so. Green stalk with purple blotches." Pip gently folded the leaves up in the cloth and hid them under the mule's lip, "I hope nothing seeps through to poison you," she said, lowering Dentata's lip around the package.

"My darling child, I am immune to hemlock. I ate a whole plant back in the day. A bit of a runny bottom for a day or two but that's not so rare for a mule."

Pip laughed and jumped back up onto Dentata's back. "Can we not go so fast on the return journey? My legs are like jelly."

The pair made their way past Octavius' farm at a far gentler pace. Pip eyed his purple grapes, glinting in the sun.

"He wouldn't miss a few bunches, would he?" She pulled gently on the reins signalling Dentata to stop. She flung her leg over the mule's hindquarters and jumped down.

"Alright, but be quick. We don't want any trouble, not now we've come so far."

Pip dipped into the gully and swiftly twisted two huge bunches of grapes from the vine. She ran back to Dentata and vaulted onto her back. "Quickly then, as fast as you like."

Dentata galloped over the stony ground while Pip held the grapes tightly against her chest with one hand, and clung onto Dentata's mane with the other. When they were a safe distance from the farm, Pip shouted out;

"Hey, slow down a minute, I've had an idea." The mule slowed down to a more dignified trot, then a walk, "What is it?"

"I want to take these grapes to my mum."

"That's a bit risky, Pip. What if you are caught?"

"I'll just say Fortuna told me to. Everybody is scared of Fortuna. I bet even the biggest gladiator would tremble at the mention of her name."

"Alright then, I'll make a detour. Hold tight."

When they arrived at the gladiator's barracks, Pip could see Cassius in the ring with her mum. She jumped off Dentata and led her to the wooden fence. She looped the reins through the fence and stood to watch. Her mum held a wooden trident in her right hand and a big net in her left. She was circling the big man, making occasional jabs at him with the trident.

"Good, good, that's it. Circle away from my left hand. Don't bring your feet together or you'll lose balance. That's it, now jab, body then head, body then head. Good work, Malefica, good work."

Dentata whinnied and Cassius looked up. He noticed Pip leaning against the fence. He recognised her as the young slave boy who returned his shield to him and gave a friendly wave. "Carry on with your footwork drills," he said to Carrie before bounding over.

"What brings you here little fellah? On a message from Marcus?" Cassius bent low to ruffle Pip's hair.

"Not today, Cassius. I'm here because Fortuna asked me to bring these grapes to Malefica. She has placed rather a large bet on her winning. She um… she blessed the grapes for luck. I'll have to speak directly to her though, in private, if you don't mind. I have an incantation I learned by heart. I must chant it with her briefly. Just so everything works, you know?"

"Of course. She needs all the luck she can find. She's doing very well though. See how she's out with me in the midday sun while all the other lazy sods are having their siesta? She's an excellent student but Crispus is such a mountain of a man, I'm terribly worried." He paused to rub his chin. "Still, that Fortuna has sent some powerful men to their knees with that hoodoo of hers. She's a bewitching one alright."

Cassius turned away from Pip and whistled for her mum to come over. "I'll leave you together for a few minutes but don't keep her for too long. Just in case the magic doesn't work, she needs some hard graft to fall back on. I'll go and fetch us both a drink. It's thirsty work, fighting."

Cassius jogged away and Carrie arrived at the fence with a red, sweaty face.

"I thought it was you. Are you alright?" She held out her hand and touched Pip's cheek.

"Yes, I'm fine. You looked quite impressive out there."

"Well, it's do or die, as they say." Carrie shrugged her shoulders and sighed.

"I brought you these." Pip handed over the grapes. "Eat them, they're delicious. I stole them from Octavius' vines."

"That should make them taste all the sweeter then. He's a horrible man."

They both stuffed the grapes into their mouths until there was juice running down their chins. Dentata scraped her hoof along the ground.

"I'm glad you found Dentata when you got here," Pip said to her mum.

"Ahem… it's Jane, actually, Jane Jones, to be precise," the mule butted in.

"Yes, if only I hadn't been stupid enough to get caught, you wouldn't have had to come here to rescue me. I wish I hadn't hatched that stupid plan with Mrs Higgins. I feel so guilty putting you in the thick of it."

"Well, I'm here now. What's done can't be undone. Anyway," Pip went on, "Dentata, Jane, I mean, it seems funny calling you that," she paused to pat the mule's neck, "Dentata is helping us and we have a plan to save you."

"Are you taking me away now? Are we going to run for it?"

"No, Cassius is on his way back. Look, here he comes, make it seem as if you're praying. Here, take my hands in yours and hum; that's it." She lowered her voice before continuing. "We're going to put something in Crispus' drink before the fight. Something that will send him to sleep."

"But how will you…?"

"Shoosh, keep humming. That's for me to worry about."

Cassius strode over carrying two wooden cups of water. "Has the spell been cast? Good stuff, now come on, Malefica, get this down you then let's practice throwing the net."

Fifteen

"How good of you to bless us with your presence," Spurius' face was more red than usual. He had several grubby tea towels over his arm and the kitchen was filled with steam. "Here, pass the piglets, would you, they need to go into the oven." Pip did as she was told, trying not to look at them. Spurius had stuffed an apple into each of their gaping mouths. She shuddered.

"Oh, do stop dithering; give them to me quickly." He snatched the tray from Pip. He was flustered. "Have you seen the peacock? His neck needs wringing. Do that for me, would you? Save you getting under my feet in here. I saw him in the garden a few minutes ago."

"No need, I've already done it." Marcus entered the cramped kitchen, a tangle of blue and green feathers draped over his arm. He threw the dead bird onto the work surface, the once majestic animal reduced to a floppy but shining mess.

"I was hoping she'd let it live, Spurius, but she insisted I kill it. Nearly broke my heart…"

"Oh, you're a sentimental old thing. I was going to kill it myself but the flaming thing went walkies, didn't it? The kids had been tormenting it so off it went, but never mind, Madam likes her meat pink and tasteless."

Marcus shrugged his shoulders then turned to leave.

Spurius started to pluck the bird, wrestling with the feathers until they were finally torn away from the body. Pip picked one up and marvelled at its markings.

"No, leave those, Pip, I need them for the garnish." He took the feather from her. "Here, take these lamps and place them under the seats in the dining room." He reached under the counter and pulled out six small oil lamps. He handed them to Pip who put them on a tray.

"Are they full? If not, fill them from the oil jug."

She picked up each lamp in turn, giving them a swish. They were made of clay and each had a bunch of grapes moulded around the handle. Only one was empty so she did as she was told and topped it up from the jug. She left the kitchen with her laden tray and made her way to the dining room which opened out into the far end of the garden. She found Quinta in there, plumping up a fat feather mattress on one of the three wide stone benches.

"Ah, hello, Pip. You've fetched my lamps; good boy. Can you put them into the spaces under the benches? That's it."

Quinta moved onto the next bench, giving its mattress a good whack and sending a cloud of dust into the air. Pip picked up the little oil lamps and tucked them into the small shelves that had been dug into the seating.

"Here, put a few drops of this perfume into each one. Be careful though, only a tiny bit in each. It's very precious."

"What is it?"

"I'm not sure. Fortuna sold it to us. She said it has magical powers but as long as it masks the stink of greedy, sweaty drunk men, then that's fine by me."

Pip took the perfume pot from her, and bending down, carefully let two beads of oil drip into each lamp. The oil smelled musky, making her sneeze. She pinched her nose until the tickle went away.

"Quinta…"

"Yes, what is it?"

"You want to marry Marcus, don't you?"

"That's the plan. In ten years' time, we will both have earned our freedom and we'll be at liberty to marry. Why do you ask?" Quinta stopped what she was doing, surprised by Pip's questions.

"I probably shouldn't say this. I don't want to get into trouble. "

"Go on; we're alone. You can talk."

"I heard Gaius. At the baths. He was talking to Octavius and

Stephanus about Marcus. He was telling them how he had no intention of giving him his freedom. He said he was going to keep him until he was an old man and fit for nothing. I tried to tell Marcus, but he got angry with me. And Spurius…"

Quinta sat down with a thump.

"Are you sure that's what you heard?"

"Yes."

Quinta leant forwards and placed her head in her hands. "Then we are working towards nothing. I mean, ten years is a long time in the future. It might be too late to have a family of our own but at least there was a light at the end of the tunnel. We work so hard for these people and what for?"

"You work hard for us because you're a SLAVE!" Lucius appeared from behind a column. He had been listening. "I'm TELLING," he shouted. "I will have you both whipped for impertinence. Fancy discussing your status so brazenly like that. DADDY! DADDY!" he yelled, his face becoming red with rage.

"Your daddy isn't home, young man," Spurius had heard the shouting and came to investigate, "And what are you doing out of your room? You were ordered by Marcus to stay there until he'd decided how to punish you. Get back in there at once. As if I don't have enough to do preparing for the dinner party." He grabbed Lucius by his ear and hauled him away from the dining room and across the garden. The boy's howling became fainter as they entered the house.

"I'm sorry," Pip said. "It looks like I've got us all into trouble now."

"Don't worry. I will speak to Marcus about it later. Maybe Gaius wasn't being serious. I'm pleased you told me anyway. Come and help me chop the cabbages. We have a mountain to get through and not much time before the guests arrive."

Pip and Quinta prepared all the vegetables in the garden.

"I'll be glad never to see another cabbage in this lifetime," Quinta said, stretching her arms out in front of her. "Pity me now, though; I have to go and help Madam Decima dress for this evening. She can be, how can I put it? She can be rather demanding."

"How long have you been a slave here?" Pip asked, piling cabbage onto a tray, "For the Ambustus family, I mean."

"Long enough," Quinta rose, brushing vegetable peelings from her tunic. "Take those in to Spurius. They'll be using you later to serve. Be careful. Don't drop anything or there'll be Hades to pay. And most importantly, make sure you're seen and not heard."

Pip followed her into the house with the tray. There was a commotion in the hall. She stayed at the kitchen entrance so she could hear what was going on. She heard Marcus' voice. He was angry.

"The boy stole something extremely valuable, Gaius, and then lied about it."

"But I didn't, Daddy, I swear." Pip heard Lucius' reedy objection.

"Not now, Lucius, I am talking to Marcus. You'll have your say later."

"He stole from a slave, darling," Pip heard Decima drawl. "That's hardly the same as stealing from a citizen."

"With respect, Madam, Cassius might be a slave, but he is a well-respected gladiator in this town and furthermore, he is a good friend of mine."

"He's right, darling; what Lucius did was shameful, and he must be punished."

"Lucius was VERY keen to point out how bad it was that Malefica stole from the Satri family. Don't you remember, Lucius?" Marcus reminded the boy what he had said in the cart.

"But I didn't DO it." Lucius had started to cry.

"You are now comparing my son with an escaped slave who broke into a house to steal. To steal from good people. I won't have it, Gaius. I know Marcus thinks he runs this house but…"

"Steady on now, darling, I don't think Marcus meant…" Gaius interrupted.

"The boy did a very bad thing, and he needs to be punished. In my opinion, he should miss the games." Marcus was firm.

"The annual games? The highlight of the year? Why, that's preposterous!" Decima exclaimed.

"He stole from Cassius. I don't think he should be allowed to show

124

his face in that arena when Cassius is fighting. If it wasn't for Tiberia, he'd be fighting without his special shield. It's not a joke in there. My friend is fighting to the death."

"I hear what you're saying, my man." Gaius edged over to Marcus and put an arm around his shoulder. "How about we compromise? What if we allow Lucius to attend the games but make him sit with the slaves?" Marcus took a few moments to think.

"Alright, the new slave boy can watch over him, but he must NOT leave his side. I want him hidden away from the gladiators."

"Smashing! I knew we could sort this out. Lucius, go back to your room and darling, you must get ready; the guests will be here soon."

Pip nipped back into the kitchen. She really didn't need Lucius trailing after her in the amphitheatre, not when she was trying to free her mother. Obstacles, always obstacles…

"Are you still faffing about, boy?" Spurius interrupted Pip's thoughts. "Put the cabbages down on the latrine top. I need you to take the wine and goblets out. You'll be in charge of drinks tonight, Pip. Please don't spill anything on the guests."

In two trips, Pip had taken two jugs of wine and six silver goblets out to the dining room. She returned to the kitchen just as the doorbell clanged.

"Jupiter save us! They're here already." Spurius was in a state of high anxiety. "Help me plate these up, would you?"

The cook took a tray from the oven. On it were a dozen dormice. They had each been stuffed with a prune and then roasted. "Cut me twelve chunks of bread about this big," He held his middle finger five centimetres from his thumb, "and scoop out a mouse-sized hole. That's it. Pop one inside so it looks like it's sleeping in a nest. Then put the mice in their nests on a serving platter. Those ones there, the posh ones."

Another two platters had been prepared on which whole baby octopi shared a bed of lettuce with boiled and halved hen's eggs. Spurius leant over his creation and let a pearl of sweat fall from the end of his nose onto a circle of egg yolk, darkening its centre. He didn't seem to notice.

"Have you finished the mice? Good boy. Take those into the dining room and put them on the centre table. And be careful, please."

The doorbell clanged again while Pip was taking the starters to the dining room. 'Be seen and not heard' echoed in her head. Without looking up, she gently placed the platter on the table.

"Ah, what have we here? If it's not the new Ambustus house-boy. Have you met him yet, darling?" Octavius turned to Valentina, his wife.

"Oh, leave the boy alone. Let him do his work. Decima will be out shortly to entertain us."

"He's a right villain this one. Tried to run away at the auction. Didn't you, young man?" Pip tried to ignore him and turned to leave.

"What do you have there for us? Hmm…? What are they?" Reluctantly, Pip turned back.

"Roast dormice, sir," she said. "Can I help you to one?" She lifted the platter and held it for Octavius to take one.

"Bred by my good self, these little beasts. Delicious but so many bones." Octavius had sucked the flesh from a dormouse and spat the bones onto the floor.

"Oh darling, really. Do you have to make such a mess? We've only just arrived." Octavius ignored his wife. "Any chance of a goblet of wine, boy? One could die of thirst around here."

Pip filled a goblet of wine and handed it to him.

"Jolly good. Another one of mine. Fabulous bouquet. Fill one for my wife." Pip did as she was told, then scuttled back to the kitchen to collect the other platters.

When she returned to the dining room, Octavius had been joined by Stephanus and a large bearded man she didn't recognise. She offered round goblets of wine to the new guests.

"Stephanus, you must remember Remus," Octavius said, rising from his bench.

"Of course. How are you, my good man? It's been a while though. How have you been?" The two men shook hands and briefly embraced.

"I can't complain. The Gods are being good to me in the main.

Apart from the water supply, that is. What a damned nuisance. Will I see you at the games? My man is fighting."

"So I heard," Stephanus said. "He'll have an easy time of it, I'm sure. He's fighting that woman Octavius bought. Is that right? Malefica? Is that what you've called her, Octavius?"

"Don't you two be so sure that your one-armed Crispus will slice her in two. Not without a fight, anyway. She has grit." Octavius paused to make fists and shake them at his friends.

"May I remind you that Crispus has fifty scalps under his belt? All of them taken at big events." Remus had been piqued.

"An ever-expanding belt, my man. Your man is past it, I'm afraid to say. How old is he? He must be thirty-five if he's a day; a slow lumbering creature. I've seen him in your fields, huffing and puffing like a geriatric carthorse. Anyway, I plan to take a whole lot of money from you all in bets." Valentina tutted and shook her head.

"You men are all the same. You never grow up. Thank Jupiter, here comes Decima. Some female company at last. Decima, darling, you look amazing."

Decima appeared on Gaius' arm. She wore a dark green stola and her auburn hair had been carefully coiled onto the top of her head and held with a gold clasp. She wore green eye shadow and Quinta had painted her lips a bright orange. She bowed her head whilst her guests admired her.

"Thank you all so much for coming," she purred.

"Yes, good to see you all, chaps. I'm so excited to be hosting this year's games." Gaius added, "Don't hang about, though, sit down and relax. Where's the boy? Fill the goblets. A toast. A toast to the most exciting games of the century!"

Pip left the dining room to the sound of clanking goblets. She had to help Spurius with the main course. She hated hearing her mother talked about in that way. It made her feel helpless.

"I know it was you." Lucius stopped her in the passage. She tried to brush past him.

"Not so fast. I knew it was you who put the shield under my bed."

"I don't know what you're talking about." Pip was cross. She was worried about her mum and she had work to do.

"Because of you, I have lost my seat on the front row. Because of you, I have to sit with all the smelly slaves at the back. I will miss everything."

"You should have thought about that before you stole from Cassius then, shouldn't you?"

Lucius flew into a rage. He grabbed Pip by the shoulders and started to shake her.

"THAT'S ENOUGH!" Marcus had been working late and had just arrived home. He seized Lucius by the collar of his tunic and lifted him into the air.

"Not only will you be watching the games with the slaves, you'll be chained to one. I am going to chain you to Pip by the ankle. You're a snivelling, spoiled brat and it's about time you were taught a lesson."

With Lucius still held aloft, Marcus barged through his bedroom screens and dropped him onto his bed.

"Don't ever let me hear you mention the games again!" He left the bedroom and turned to Pip, saying, "Right then, let's serve the pigs to the pigs."

Sixteen

The tray of piglets was too heavy for Pip to carry on her own. Spurius left the haven of his kitchen to take them for her. Pip carried the dinner plates. She'd already taken the peacock in. Spurius had attached its blue and green uncooked head back onto its neck and had stuck a spray of shimmering feathers in its backside.

Octavius by this point was reclining on one of the benches whilst the other guests sat side by side.

"Ah, Spurius," Gaius said, "Those look wonderful. I must say, you surpassed yourself with the first course."

"Thank you, sir. I always aim to please." Octavius started to snigger.

"It's a rare thing, a flabby slave. His tunic barely fits over the podge. Whoever heard of such a thing?" He swivelled his head to face Valentina. "We have the slimmest slaves in Pompeii, wouldn't you say, darling? We don't spoil them. What's the point?"

"Thank you, Spurius, that will be all," Gaius rose from his bench and ushered the cook out into the garden. "Send Marcus in, would you? I'd like him to join us for a bite to eat. He's been a bit tetchy for a day or two. I don't know what's wrong with him."

"See?" Octavius continued, "That's what happens when you spoil your slaves. They start to think they're one of us. They take offence when they remember their inferior birth and the consequences of being a nobody."

"Oh, darling, do hold your tongue; please don't sour another evening. It's a habit he has, Gaius; I apologise on his behalf."

"Ah, there's no need to apologise, my dear Valentina. I've known Octavius for many years. He's a cantankerous old stick and we love

129

him for it. Where's the boy? Fill up Octavius' goblet. A few more swigs will soften his edges."

"He needs more water with his wine if you ask me." Valentina cast a glance at her husband and tutted.

Pip did as she was told, just as Marcus appeared at the dining room entrance. He had mud on his white tunic.

"You called for me, sir?"

Gaius stepped out and leant against a stone column. "Yes, come and join us for dinner. I'd like to thank you for your help with the games. You've worked so very hard. I couldn't have done it without you."

"I've been trying to fix the water fountain, sir. It's not working." He held the spout in his hand, a peacock head.

"My peacock fountain, Marcus. You promised," Decima complained.

"Maybe you should have let the real peacock live. There's nothing more beautiful than a living peacock. There's plenty of other food to eat. I was very sorry when you asked me to kill it." Marcus raised his voice so Decima could hear him properly.

"Gaius, are you going to let him talk to me like that?"

"Anyway," Marcus went on, "there's nothing I can do, Madam. I connected the pipe to the water barrel, but the pressure is too low. I can only apologise."

"I must insist that you try again." Decima stood up from the bench she shared with Valentina. "It really is very important that I have the fountain working tonight."

Marcus sighed and headed back towards the end of the garden.

"I'm having the same trouble on my farm," said Remus, becoming animated. "The well is remarkably low. My slaves are having to fetch water from the pool by the olive grove. It's such a long way from the town though, and Bacchus only knows how long it will be before that dries up. Can't you do anything, Gaius? You are the senator, after all."

"I would if I could, my good man. Sadly, I cannot control the elements. I'm sure it will right itself soon enough. We are good people, us Pompeiians. The Gods will remember us in no time. I suggest we all say some extra prayers."

"What piffle. Praying won't make a blind bit of difference. You'll be wasting your time. Never been one for mumbo-jumbo, me…" Octavius had started to slur his words.

Gaius continued undeterred, "The Ambustus family will be having a special ceremony before the games, just at our humble shrine, here at home. Hopefully, Bacchus will hear us and help us. Why, he's probably busy with a particularly good flagon of wine. As soon as he sobers up, I'm sure he'll persuade the water to flow again."

"Yes, whatever," Octavius made a dismissive gesture in the air with his hand, "Can we chow down now? I'm starving. Where's the boy? Lurking in the shadows? Fetch me some of that pig."

The dining room fell silent for a while as the guests gorged themselves. Pip was on hand to fill up wine goblets which she did frequently. Eventually, Marcus returned, again with the peacock spout in his hand.

"I'm sorry, it's no use."

Decima exhaled loudly and jutted out her bottom lip in the same way Lucius did when he was about to have a tantrum. Gaius was keen to avoid any such outburst from his wife.

"Never mind, Decima, I'll make it up to you, I promise. Where's the boy? Get Marcus a full plate and fill a goblet for him. That's enough work for today; come and join us."

"It's alright, sir, I have some admin to finish tonight and there really isn't any room for me on the benches." He placed the peacock head on the table and turned to leave.

"Octavius," Valentina chided, "If you sat up, Marcus could sit beside you. You're taking up a whole bench. That really is rather selfish."

"You expect me to dine with a slave? Really…"

"Yes, I do. This is Gaius' home, and you will respect the way he lives. Sit yourself up and stop being such a baby."

Octavius reluctantly sat up. As he did, he slopped half a goblet of wine down his toga.

"That must be why you are so fond of wearing purple, old boy," Gaius laughed.

"What in the name of Jupiter has the world come to where a citizen of Pompeii is forced to dine with a slave?"

'Oh, stop making a fuss," Valentina said. "You're making a spectacle of yourself. Sit yourself down, Marcus, and ignore the old fool. And tell us, what do you have lined up for the Pompeiian people at the games tomorrow? That's the reason we're here, after all, a dinner to welcome in the annual games. I'm tremendously excited for you."

"Thank you, Madam Valentina. Yes, we've put in a lot of hard work. I hope the games reflect well on Master Gaius."

"Your first year as senator. How do you think it has gone?" Remus asked.

"We'll find out soon enough," Octavius slurred. "The elections are looming."

"My husband has been an excellent senator so far. He's done it all by himself, without one iota of help from anyone. Haven't you, darling?"

Decima's words made Marcus shift uneasily in his seat. Gaius noticed and said, "I couldn't have done anything without my right-hand man. Could I, Marcus? Tell everyone what we've got for them tomorrow."

Marcus took a sip of wine and spoke slowly. "Well, we will begin with the animals, I think, just to warm things up. We have imported some large animals from Africa. That took some organisation, I can tell you."

"Smashing," Remus said. "What do you have? Any elephants? I always thought I could use one of those on my farm; enormous sturdy beasts they are."

"Not this year, sir, I'm afraid. We thought about it, but we don't have the water volume for elephants. They are thirsty creatures."

"We have some big cats and some interesting prey, don't we, Marcus? There's also a mountain of interesting dung piling up in the amphitheatre. I should give you some for your roses, Octavius. Tell them what else we have, Marcus."

"I think we'll have a brief interval after the animals, followed by some amateur bouts, just to break up the intensity."

"Not to be ignored either," Gaius piped up. "This is where we are to be introduced to the gladiator giants of the future; a showcase, if you like."

"You mean you rounded up a rabble of thieves and petty criminals? I know you; you're forever doing things on the cheap."

The conversation was disturbed by Spurius who had appeared with another silver platter. "I have pudding, Master Gaius. Pip, can you gather the dirty plates from the table?"

"What have you made for us?" Gaius asked.

"Baked figs in honey, sir," he said, putting the platter onto the table before heading back to the kitchen with the dirty plates.

"This is delicious," Valentina said. "Please go on, Marcus; what else is happening tomorrow?"

"I don't know why you are interested," Octavius said, rubbing honey dribble from his chin. "Strictly no women at the games. Isn't that right, Gaius? It's the law."

"They are MY games, and I will invite whomever I like. I'm a modern man, my friend. Anyway, we need Valentina there to keep an eye on you."

"I'm sick to death of mothering my husband, Gaius, but thank you; of course, I'd love to come. Carry on, Marcus, please."

"After the amateur bouts, Malefica will be fighting Crispus, but I'm still not sure it's such a good idea."

"I also had reservations about this, I must admit," Gaius said, "but I promised Octavius."

"What are you two on about? That fight is the talk of the town. What could be more entertaining than a daring female cat burglar facing a retired one-armed giant in a fight to the death?"

"Well, when you put it like that, I suppose it DOES sound like a jolly old lark," Gaius laughed.

He said this just as Pip was filling up Octavius' goblet. She wobbled and spilled more wine down his toga.

"Oh, give it here, damned fool!" Octavius bellowed and snatched the wine jug from her. Pip slunk away, humiliated.

"Then, after that contest, we have the headline fight. My good friend and true warrior, Cassius, will be fighting Maximus."

"Who is this Maximus fellow?" Remus asked, "Does he have form?"

"He's the Roman champion, sir. He's fairly new to the game but he has climbed the ranks quickly. He's a good, solid fighter. A captured soldier I believe, and it shows."

"If he was that good a fighter, he wouldn't have been caught," Octavius butted in. Marcus ignored him. "I hope Cassius finds a way to defeat him. I believe in my friend's strength and skill, but this will be a tough fight for him."

"The tougher the better," Octavius was now swaying in his seat. "The tougher and more drawn out the better. Nobody wants to see a quick, clean finish. We want blood and lots of it."

"Forgive me, sir, but I disagree. It's good to see talent and strength but gore and pain are not the goals here. Gladiators are human beings and should be respected as such."

"I'm amazed you don't shed a tear over the animals ripped to shreds too. Your heart is quick to bleed for that of a slave."

"With respect, sir, slaves are also human beings, and you're right, I don't find pleasure in cruelty of any sort. Unfortunately, it seems to be what the people of Pompeii want to see, and I have no say in the matter." Marcus stood up, towering over Octavius. "Because, as you have made it clear, I am merely a slave and a slave has no worth, and therefore, no opinion."

"Sit down, Marcus, there's no need to get heated," Gaius said. "I think everyone is a bit tired and emotional this evening."

"You're right and my husband has drunk far too much wine."

"It's free, isn't it, darling? Gaius is very generous with my phenomenal vino. Isn't it amazing though? I grow the grapes and ferment the wine, bottle it up, sell it to our outstanding senator friend here, then get to drink it. It's hilarious…"

"You made Gaius PAY for our wine, Octavius? Knowing that you'd be drinking a fair portion of it yourself? You really are a parsimonious little man. I am thoroughly ashamed of you. You've always been a miser. I don't know why I married you."

"I am nothing of the sort," Octavius shook his head violently. "I am a generous man. I'm probably the most generous man in the city of Pompeii."

Stephanus and Remus started to laugh. "That's pushing it a bit, old boy; you're always the last to open his purse in the tavern," Gaius said. "In fact, I've never seen you open your purse."

"I suppose you think you're the most benevolent man in the land in hosting these games, Senator Gaius."

"Actually, Octavius, they have been rather costly."

"Don't pretend that there haven't been some dodgy deals going on. I know what happens at the forum; you scratch my back, I'll scratch yours."

"I won't deny there's been a small contribution from sponsors, but most of the money for the games has come out of my own pocket. You could have made a contribution yourself, my friend."

"I gave you Malefica, didn't I? She cost me a few quid."

"You paid peanuts for her, old boy. Why not put your money where your mouth is? It's not as if you're short of a bob or two."

"Alright then. Here's an idea. Because I am going to be in receipt of a giant windfall from good old Remus here when my girl wins, I will buy the freedom of any gladiator left standing at the close of the games. I give you permission to make the announcement. Fetch me a scroll and I will seal it." Remus started to laugh.

"You haven't got a hope in hell, my dear man. You're making a fool of yourself. Your 'girl' is a street urchin captured by the state for burgling houses. She's only had five minutes of training. My man has killed over fifty men in the amphitheatre. You really have lost your mind. Still, if it's easy money for me, I salute your idiocy."

"Nonsense, my simple sheep-breeding bumpkin. Malefica is fresh. She's fresh and eager to win. She'll fight like a dog in that arena. She'll put your lumbering oaf to shame. Your lumbering 'one-armed' oaf, I might add. Also, freedom upon victory is a marvellous incentive, don't you think?"

"More of an incentive than keeping her life? You really have no idea, do you?" Marcus got up from his seat. "I can't listen to any more of this. It's just amusement for you, playing with peoples' lives. I'm sorry, sir; thank you for this evening. I will go and finish my work. I'll see you all at the games tomorrow." He made a short bow towards the rest of the guests. "Don't leave it too late though, Master Gaius," he added. "Tomorrow is a big day."

"Thank Jupiter for that. He FINALLY took the hint," Octavius spluttered. "It's terribly poor form to mix with subordinates. The manner in which he speaks to citizens is shocking. His own master's friends, in fact."

"He doesn't mean it. He's tired. He's probably not had much sleep over the last few weeks," Gaius said.

"My dear husband, you need to be told some home truths sometimes. And anyway, you've done it now; you're going to regret that promise you made when you sober up tomorrow. I wonder how much Cassius' owners will charge you for his freedom."

"We shall see, we shall see."

"And you'll let Malefica go if she wins?" Decima asked. "What if she goes on to burgle more houses?"

"Oh, I think she'll have learned her lesson. Look, Gaius, now we've got rid of Marcus, can we get rid of the women too? It's time they left the men to discuss important matters. They can't be expected to make a reasonable contribution to after-dinner discourse, not with their inferior little brains. A man needs to recline with other men at this juncture; in fact, I insist."

"Valentina's brain is clearly as sharp as yours, my good fellow," Gaius said, "if not sharper, especially now you've got yourself sozzled on that wine of yours."

"Don't worry, Gaius, Decima and I can talk in her room. We have a lot to catch up on. When he becomes unconscious, would you put my husband in the cart and send him home? Thank you." Valentina rose, took hold of Decima's hand and led her out of the dining room.

Seventeen

The next morning, Pip arrived at Dentata's stable before the sun had come up. She raised the latch and went inside.

"Oh, you have a friend."

Dentata exhaled loudly, "Yes, this is Ovid. He's not the brightest, bless him, and he's tiny. I hope he's up to the job." Pip pushed past Dentata to stroke the new mule. His coat was the colour of mushroom soup and he had a black line running down his back. "His ears are enormous," Pip said, giving them a gentle tug.

"Yes, I think there's more donkey in him than Marcus was led to believe. But I'm sure he'll grow into those big hairy lugs and I'm sure Tiberia will grow to love him as much as she loves me."

"Yes, I hope so. He's very sweet." Pip patted his neck.

"The slaughterman is coming tomorrow and Tiberia's been beside herself. I'm very worried about her."

"Oh Dentata! I forgot. I am so sorry. Are you sure it's what you want? Will it hurt? Are you sure you want to be human again? We're a pretty horrible lot, after all. I could open the stable door and you could run to the hills."

"Look at Ovid here. Not very inspiring, is he? Would you like to live out your days chewing vegetable peelings and swishing flies away from your backside with your tail?"

"No, I suppose not."

"I'm coming home with you. I'm coming back to London as a human being. I have a bone to pick with Toothless, if nothing else."

"Hey! Look what I have," Pip said. She opened up her hand to reveal a small silver pot.

"That looks expensive. What is it?"

"I stole it from Decima's room just now. I dug out the eyeshadow. Look, it even has a little silver stick for mixing."

"Oh, I see. You'd better take this then. You'll need it today. But be careful not to get any of it on your hands."

Dentata curled back her top lip so Pip could retrieve the hemlock. "Ew, it's all soggy."

"I apologise for the mule drool. Now, hurry on in, as you have a long day ahead of you."

"I wish I wasn't so tired, Dentata. I've not been to sleep at all. I was up all night serving the men at the dinner party."

"Yes, I heard them. What a vulgar man Octavius is. Anyway, run along. And good luck. Oh, and Pip?"

"Yes?"

"Don't forget to tell your mum about Fortuna's house in Misenum."

"I won't. See you later."

After she had finished the rest of her morning chores, Pip met Marcus and Spurius in the kitchen. Marcus was holding court, trying not to let his nerves get the better of him.

"I think everything is in place. The canvas awnings have already been taken to the amphitheatre; Quinta fixed all the rips. Spurius can take the food up in the cart. Listen, I can hear the family assembling in the hall. Spurius, you finish up here. Pip, come with me. You are in charge of Lucius today."

Pip and Marcus stood discreetly by the front door. They watched as Gaius led his family through the corridor, into the hall and over to the shrine. They were wearing the lavish clothes Pip had helped collect from Stephanus the fuller.

The master of the house looked majestic in his purple-edged toga. Pride was holding his head high in the air and he puffed out his chest like a triumphant cockerel.

Decima wore her hair curled over the top of her head. Quinta had fastened it with a brooch made from shells and she wore two peacock feathers that seemed to be growing out of her ears.

Her face was painted a brilliant white and her lips were the colour of pomegranate seeds. Pip hoped she hadn't missed her eye shadow pot. She nervously felt for it under her swimsuit. It now contained the hemlock paste she had prepared by grinding the leaves up with olive oil.

Lucius and Tiberia followed behind. They were more plainly dressed in white tunics, but Tiberia had insisted that Quinta curled her hair to look like her mother's.

"My beloved family," Gaius began, "Let us pray to Bacchus. We need his blessings for the day ahead. Come, children, gather round." The family made a semi-circle around the shrine, the centrepiece being the god himself riding a sleek black marble panther. Various offerings had been laid out by Spurius - a pot of honey, some nuts and figs.

He had also left out four silver goblets and a jug of wine. Decima poured out the wine and passed the goblets to her family.

"Almighty Bacchus, hear our prayer," she cried out quite suddenly. Tiberia giggled. Lucius elbowed her. Decima took a large swig of wine before she continued; "Powerful and most accomplished Bacchus, our lips are stained with your life-giving blood. Hear us this day, your faithful servants. We pray that you bless our games."

She paused to take another slug of wine, leaving a red lipstick stain on the goblet.

"And while you're at it, dear Bacchus," Gaius beseeched, "please turn the water back on. The people of Pompeii are very upset about it all."

Decima drained her goblet.

"Decima, darling, steady on, the wine is an offering for the Gods; you're not supposed to drink it all.

The rest of the family placed their full goblets of wine back onto the shrine.

"Are you ready to go, sir? I think it's time," Marcus called over from the front door.

The two slaves stood aside to let the family pass out of the house.

"Not so fast!" Marcus grabbed Lucius by the shoulders to stop him leaving. "You will be spending the day with Pip. Had you forgotten?"

"You said I had to stay with the slaves at the amphitheatre. You didn't mention the procession."

"You will be travelling with Pip in the cart."

"I'd rather eat worms than go anywhere with the household skivvy."

"I can't say I'm thrilled about it either," Pip shrugged.

"How DARE you answer back," Lucius shouted.

Gaius came back into the house looking agitated.

"What's going on here? What's the hold-up?"

"Lucius had forgotten the terms of his punishment, Master Gaius."

"Oh, Lucius, not today, please. I have enough on my plate as it is."

"But the GAMES, Daddy."

"It's one games of many you will experience in your lifetime. Just behave like a grown-up and accept it, please. Do as Marcus says. I will see you later." Gaius hurried back out of the front door.

"I can't believe Tiberia will get to see everything while I'm stuck with the stinky slave. It's not FAIR!"

"Listen, Lucius," Marcus bent low to speak directly into the boy's face. "You're lucky you're going at all. If I had my way, you'd be spending the day in Dentata's stable, sitting in her turds."

"Wait until I tell my Mummy what you just said."

"Your mummy isn't interested right now. She's currently parading her fancy self through the streets of Pompeii, with every citizen's eye upon her. Now come on; the cart is waiting."

Spurius was waiting outside the front door with the new mule.

"What's that thing? That's far too small to pull the cart. You might as well get the slave to pull it."

"Just get in, Lucius. I need to run ahead and catch the family. See you later, Spurius."

"Right, you two, jump in," the cook said.

"It's alright, I'll walk alongside you," Pip said, "Ovid does look a little bit small to pull us both."

"Have you got the whip? That usually works for lazy mules."

"Sit DOWN, Lucius, please."

The cart rolled on. Spurius held Ovid's harness and Pip stroked

140

his neck as she walked. Lucius sulked at the back of the cart, jutting his lip out, before suddenly becoming animated. He squeezed past the huge pile of food to the front of the cart, making Ovid stumble.

"I hope there are elephants this year. Spurius, are there going to be elephants?"

"No, I don't think so, Master Lucius."

"Why not? The elephants are my favourite. Do you remember last year? There were twelve of them. Two were killed by lions I think, and the rest were ANNIHILATED by the gladiators. That was just the BEST bit. They made a fantastic din when they were slaughtered."

"That sounds horrible. They must have been in a lot of pain," Pip said through clenched teeth.

"Who asked you? And Spurius, do you remember those birds? What are they called? I think they come from Africa?"

"I'm not so sure Master Lucius. I'm usually too busy working to watch the games."

"Ostriches, that's what they're called. They are REALLY funny. They have long thin necks and teeny tiny heads. They were running round the arena in all directions. There were loads of them. Then - and this was the best bit - the gladiators came into the ring." Pip groaned.

"Shut up, you, it was ace. The ostriches were frantic, bumping into each other. Then they scattered trying to escape, so the gladiators spread out and started to pick them off one by one, slicing their heads off with those sharp discs they threw as they ran. It was FANTASTIC!"

"It can't be good for you, watching all that gore at your age," Spurius said.

"Why not? It's so much fun. My favourite gladiator, after Cassius, of course, who is my VERY best favourite, was the one with one eye. Do you remember him? I think he might have died. Daddy said he lost his eye because a tiger slashed his face. Is that true?"

"I'm not sure. I heard someone took a gladiator's eye out with a tip of a sword, but I think the unfortunate fellow was called Titus. You might be confusing him with Crispus, the one who lost his arm in a lion's mouth. Remember him?"

"Um… maybe. Is he dead? Did the lion eat the rest of him too?"

"No, no, Crispus didn't die, he just retired. You'll see him today; he's making a special appearance. He's been brought out of retirement to fight Malefica."

"The slave we took to the barracks? I held her in the cart. I tied her wrists." Pip stiffened at the mention of her mother.

"She's the woman who burgled the Satri house. Octavius bought her and concocted this crazy idea."

"I thought she'd be fighting another useless girl, which would have been rather boring."

"Well, you were wrong, Master Lucius, though it all seems pretty bawdy to me. She won't stand a chance."

"Golly, well I think it's terribly exciting. I bet he'll make short work of her. Is he massive? Most gladiators are massive. He'll kill her with just one swipe." Lucius stood up and slashed the air with his arm, "JUST… LIKE… THAT…"

"I can hear shouting," Pip said, changing the subject. "What is it?"

"That'll be the crowd at the forum. Gaius was stopping there to make a pre-games speech."

"Can we stop and listen? Can we, Spurius? Can we, please? I want to hear Daddy."

"Well…," Spurius pulled Ovid to a halt. "We'll be going in the wrong direction. It's out of our way."

"Oh, Spurius, PLEASE, can we? Please?"

"I suppose it IS a very special occasion, but we mustn't stay long. I have to get these supplies to the amphitheatre before the family arrive. I'll be in deep, deep trouble if I don't." Let me tie Ovid to that tree."

The forum square was packed full of people. Pip could just about make out Gaius' tiny figure on the forum steps. Spurius stood between Pip and Lucius, just near the gates. He held on to both of them tightly.

The crowd was humming with anticipation. The whole of Pompeii had turned out for the annual event. Gaius jumped onto an empty plinth at the foot of the forum's giant pillars. The crowd let out a roar.

"My friends," he declared as the roar became a hum once more. "Good people of Pompeii…" The crowd fell silent.

"Thank you for attending these very special games. My wife and I…" he said, looking down at Decima who shone with pride, "My wife and I are very pleased to welcome you on this beautiful day. We have been blessed by the Gods in being able to share our wealth with this great town, in financing a day of games and gladiatorial combat." Gaius looked out across the crowd with dewy eyes.

"It was my father's wish that one day, one of his sons would grow to be a man of some importance in this town and by Jove, I think I've done it."

The crowd cheered; Gaius continued his speech.

"We are especially grateful to Bacchus for blessing the soil and nurturing Pompeii's vines to provide the wine for this day of enjoyment. Let us hope that he nourished the gladiators well last night, so they come out fighting today with fire in their bellies."

The crowd roared again. Gaius waited for quiet.

"So, my friends, drink with your fellow citizens. Drink in the fruits of the vine. Enjoy all the action laid on for you and remember that I, Gaius Fabius Ambustus, am your faithful servant. To the amphitheatre!"

The crowd erupted once more into applause.

"Quick, you two, let's get going before the rabble set off." Spurius ushered Pip and Lucius back onto the road where he untied Ovid from the tree.

"I'll race you," Lucius shouted. "Last one there's a loser!" he shouted, kicking up dust with his sandals as he sped away.

Eighteen

The crowd had started to leave the forum. It oozed onto the road, around the cart. Spurius began to panic.

"Marcus is going to kill me."

"Why?" Pip was pleased to be rid of Lucius.

"He'll have my guts for garters if I've lost him. I was under strict instructions to make sure he stayed with the household slaves."

"Maybe it's for the best if he entertains himself today. You know what he's like. He's a troublemaker."

"That may be so, my dear boy, but Marcus was adamant that he was to be punished for stealing Cassius' shield."

"It seems to me that his punishment is punishment for everybody else."

"I think you might be right, young Pip, but what can we do? Rules are rules."

Pip wondered how her mum was feeling. She would be at the amphitheatre by now. She must be terrified, she thought to herself. The crowd had started to jostle the cart. Someone leaned in and stole a loaf of bread.

"Hey! Stop that!" Spurius shouted after him, shaking his head in despair. He turned to Pip, "I'm supposed to have all this food and wine set out for the family before they arrive. I wish I hadn't listened to that loathsome child."

Spurius' face was a deeper red than usual. Sweat hung from his big moustache in globules before bursting to stain his tunic. He clicked his tongue to push Ovid on.

"Don't worry. I'll have this stuff unloaded in no time."

"Thank you, Pip. You're a good boy."

"Anyway, does Marcus really need to know Lucius has run off? I won't tell him if you don't."

Spurius pulled Ovid to a halt outside the amphitheatre. Pip saw the circular stone of the amphitheatre behind the palaestra wall and shivered.

"You jump into the back and hand me down the food, would you?"

Spurius barged through a group of young men to tie Ovid to a tree. Just as he looped the leather of the reins around a small branch, he turned to face Marcus who had hold of Lucius by the shoulders.

"Honestly, Spurius, I can't trust you to keep hold of a ten-year-old boy." Marcus was angry.

"He ran off. What was I to do? Chain myself to him?"

"Funny you should say that. That's exactly what I am going to do. Hold onto him for a moment. Tightly!"

Marcus delved into the cart.

"It's in here somewhere. I used to wear it when I was new to the family, to stop me from running away. I knew it would come in handy for something one day. Ah, here it is." Marcus pulled out a heavy chain from under some rags at the back of the cart. At both ends were ankle clasps.

"You're not chaining ME to the boy," Spurius said, looking indignant.

"I should, considering it was you who let him go." Marcus smiled. "But no. Today is your lucky day. Come over here, Pip."

"You're not chaining ME to a smelly slave," Lucius suddenly piped up.

"Do you have to? Really?" Pip joined in.

"I've already told you, Lucius, if I'd had my way, you wouldn't have made it past the front door. Maybe this will help you to understand that when you steal and lie, there are consequences to be endured."

"But I didn't DO it."

"I'm sick of hearing your lies. Give me your foot."

"I won't! I…"

"Now!" Marcus bent low and grabbed Lucius' ankle, placed the clasp around it, turned the key and took it out, "Now you, Pip."

"But what about all the food that needs taking up? I promised I'd help Spurius."

"Never mind about that now. Spurius can manage by himself. Give me your foot."

Pip reluctantly did as she was told. She'd have no chance of saving her mother now, not with Lucius tethered to her leg.

"Have the gladiators arrived yet?" she asked.

"Indeed, they have," Marcus replied, turning the second key and adding it to the one already in the leather pouch on his belt.

"Are they all okay?"

"They seem to be, yes. The big cats don't look too happy though. We can't wake one of them up. Now listen, make sure Lucius doesn't get into any trouble please, Pip, and keep him away from the family. I want him to know how it feels to lose his privilege for a day. He should see things from our perspective for once."

"Here come the family now, Marcus." Spurius held his hand over his eyes to peer into the sun.

Pip jostled with Lucius to get the best view of Gaius and Decima. They appeared in the street flanked by soldiers who kept them apart from the crowd. They walked slowly and proudly, stopping occasionally to wave or say something to one of their townsfolk. As they approached the palaestra entrance of the amphitheatre, two men hurried out with gates to separate Gaius, Decima and Tiberia from the rest of the rabble.

"Tiberia looks stupid," Lucius said.

"She looks fine; you're just jealous." Pip craned her neck to see Quinta bend to pick up the hem of Decima's stola as she began the ascent of the amphitheatre steps. Marcus joined them. The family vanished inside and the gates were closed behind them.

The palaestra itself was a bustle of activity. Stalls had been set up to sell drinks and snacks. Stall holders resumed putting the finishing touches to their displays once the family had passed through.

"Well, I suppose I can still make use of you two," Spurius said. He handed Pip a flagon of wine. "There's only a tiny bit of water, I'm afraid. I had to collect some from the barrel in the kitchen. If the wine is well honeyed, hopefully, nobody will notice the absence of water."

"Lucius, take this basket of food. I'll carry the rest."

The guards, recognising Spurius, opened the gates to let them through. They had to squeeze through hordes of excited men.

"Certainly not," Lucius shouted above the din. "I may be chained to a slave but I'm not going to be used like one."

"Suit yourself," Spurius struggled on with a basket on each arm.

"Can we use this entrance?" Pip pointed to a high gated arch.

"No. That's the gladiator entrance. They are all inside now, so it's been locked. We need to take the stairs here. We're following Master Gaius."

"You're going too fast. This flagon is heavy." Lucius nearly pulled Pip over trying to race to the top of the stone staircase.

"Get a move on then, you lazy good-for-nothing."

"Lucius, stop it or the wine is going to be spilled. Do you want me to tell Marcus you made Pip spill the wine?"

Lucius settled down and fell into Pip's rhythm to climb the stairs without tripping her up. Spurius and Pip were breathless when they reached the top. They paused to rest.

Pip looked down at the great amphitheatre which had been dug deep into the ground. There were rows and rows of stone seating that climbed from the flat oval arena to the top where they were standing.

The seating areas were separated by aisles of stairs. A layer of sand covered the floor of the stadium. Again, Pip thought of her mother and felt for the hemlock under her clothes. What use was having it if she wouldn't be able to escape from Lucius? The boy spoke;

"I see the sand is thick today. They must be expecting a lot of blood; Malefica's mostly, I bet." He stabbed the air with an imaginary knife. "Lots of sand to soak up the spurting blood."

"What is that small door for? The one in the middle?" Pip asked.

"That's where they drag the dead ones out. Sometimes they have to give them a bash with a hammer, just to make sure. Oof... right on the noggin..."

"Right, you two," Spurius interrupted, "I'm going to take the food to the family before the gates are opened. Stay there for a moment and I'll be back for the wine."

"I'm thirsty," Lucius complained.

"There's nothing to drink yet apart from wine. Wait until I go back to the cart and get the posca I made for you kids."

"But I'm thirsty now!" Spurius ignored the boy and made his way to the family with his baskets. Pip had an idea.

"I bet you couldn't drink un-diluted wine. You're too young and puny."

"Is that right? Is that really what you think?"

"Yes, I do. Only grown-up men drink real wine. Grown-ups and gladiators."

"I'll be a man before you; you'll be a stunted slave-boy forever."

"If you say so. Anyway, drink the wine. I dare you."

Lucius looked at the wine flagon at Pip's feet then looked to see that Spurius was far away.

"Take the lid off then." Pip did as she was told.

"I bet you're not strong enough to lift it to your lips!"

"Of course I am. Watch me…"

Lucius bent down to pick up the heavy flagon. He hauled it up to his face.

"Go on, take a good long slug." Lucius began to drink. When he had run out of breath, he put the flagon down.

"Is that all you're having? A gladiator would have finished it off in one gulp."

Lucius picked the wine up again and guzzled some more, just as Spurius returned with the empty baskets.

"What on earth are you doing? I told you to wait for the posca."

Lucius had purple wine stains around his mouth.

"Your mother will send me to the mines for getting you drunk. What were you thinking?"

Lucius giggled, puffing out his chest. "I was thirsty. I was a thirsty gladiator!"

"I despair of you, I honestly do. Give the wine to me. Octavius is here. He's already been asking for it. The gates will be opened any second. Let me get you two seated so I can fetch the rest of the food."

Spurius picked up the wine and ushered Pip and Lucius towards the best seats in the arena. They walked across the highest tier, then made their way down the stone steps to where the family were sitting. Gaius and Decima sat on the front row and were flanked by Octavius and Valentina on one side and Stephanus and Remus on the other. Immediately behind them sat all the other important people of Pompeii, ranked in importance by how close they would be to the action.

"Why isn't my sister with Mum and Dad?" Lucius' face was flushed, and he seemed a bit unsteady on his feet.

"For some unfathomable reason, she wanted to sit with you two. She caused quite a fuss."

Spurius nudged Lucius and Pip into an empty row, about ten from the front.

"Where is my cushion?" Lucius demanded, moving his mouth around his words like a goldfish blowing bubbles. "I'm not sitting on those cold hard seats without my cushion."

"I suppose you'd like a slave to fan you too, would you?" Spurius shook his head.

"When it gets hot, yes, I would," Lucius slurred.

Marcus appeared holding Tiberia's hand. "There'll be no cushions or fans for you today, I'm afraid. You're being punished, remember? And what is wrong with you? Did you have too much sun yesterday?"

"He's has been in at the wine, I'm afraid. He snaffled some when my back was turned."

"For Jove's sake, Spurius, what were you thinking? Don't let Gaius find out whatever you do. Pip, YOU were supposed to be keeping an eye on him."

"Lucius is just very naughty sometimes," Tiberia piped up, taking Pip's hand. "I'm sure Pip is trying his best. I'd hate to be tied to my brother all day long."

"Spurius, get the kids seated, would you? The gates have just been opened."

"But there's so much to be brought out of the cart still."

"Never mind that now. Wait until Gaius does the formal opening then you can duck out."

"If you say so."

149

Marcus dashed away leaving Spurius with the children. They all sat down and waited.

Pip heard the crowd before she saw it. The noise started as a low throb, rising to an overwhelming din as the people of Pompeii filled the amphitheatre. She closed her eyes and thought of her mum. She thought of how the noise of the crowd would be terrifying to her. She felt helpless and trapped.

"Are you CRYING?" Lucius taunted. Pip wiped a tear from her cheek.

"Leave him alone," Tiberia said.

"No, I'm not crying. I have an eyelash caught in my eye."

"Why don't you go and sit with Mummy and Daddy?" Lucius bent around Pip to speak to his sister.

"Because I didn't want to be near all the blood and nastiness."

"What a waste. I could have sat there and enjoyed it. The blood is the best bit."

"Then maybe you shouldn't have stolen the shield."

"I didn't steal the shield and anyway, I wish I had a brother. Sisters are rubbish."

"Would you shut up, PLEASE?" Pip was cross. "Just sit down both of you. I think Master Gaius is about to speak."

The rowdy chatter and the constant slapping of sandals on the stone steps began to peter out. Marcus appeared again and stood in the aisle, one hand on Tiberia's shoulder.

"This is it, kids," he said, "this is really it."

A small man in a dirty tunic came hurrying towards them, taking two steps at a time.

"I'm sorry, Marcus," he blurted out. "There's a problem with the animals."

"What is it? We're about to begin."

"Well, as you know, we've been very low on water. The big cats are terribly thirsty. The sleepy one I think might actually be dead. We've been trying to fetch water from the river, but a wheel fell off one of the carts."

"That's ALL we need," Marcus groaned.

"The ostriches are fine. They're prancing around their cages, but the other cats have become as lifeless as the first. I think the animal display will have to be postponed."

"Spurius, do you think you'd be able to take our cart to the river?"

"Our cart is still full of food, remember?"

"Then take the food out."

"It's a long way to get there and back. Where are the barrels?"

Marcus turned to the grubby man;

"Take a barrel to the palaestra. Spurius can get water. We'll just have to jiggle things around a bit in the programme."

Spurius stood up and groaned. He squeezed his tummy past the children who had to stand up to let him out. Marcus clapped him on the back as he left,

"No dawdling, eh? Please, hurry back." He spoke again to the small man;

"I know what we can do," he rubbed his chin, "We can have the under-card gladiatorial bouts in place of the animals, until they have been refreshed, of course, then we can put Malefica and Crispus on. That should keep the crowd happy. We can use the animals just before the main event. We were wise not to import elephants this year, eh?"

"No elephants? Boo!" Lucius complained.

"What about the gladiators?" Marcus asked, "Are they not a bit dry?"

"They have some wine left, I think. Maybe someone can take some more down later."

"Alright, I'll sort it. Be quiet now; Gaius has just stood up."

A hush fell and all eyes focused on the amphitheatre. A herald wearing a bright orange tunic strode into the arena through a large iron gate that clanged shut behind him. He made three loud blasts on his bugle.

"Citizens of Pompeii!" he then shouted. A cheer rose from the crowd. "Citizens of Pompeii," the crowd was silent, "today's games are brought to you by Senator Gaius Fabius Ambustus." Another cheer bellowed from the aisles. "Please be upstanding for Senator Gaius!"

Nineteen

"Men of Pompeii, please be seated." Silence fell over the amphitheatre. Gaius gazed over the arena, the happiest man alive.

"I am proud to call myself a Pompeiian." The crowd cheered. "I am proud to have grown up in these streets. I am proud of you, my Pompeiian family."

"Oh, get on with it," Octavius heckled.

"Before I officially open this year's games, I have an announcement to make. I have a scroll here stating that Octavius Biblius, my good friend and local landowner, has promised to free every gladiator left standing at the close of the games." The crowd cheered.

"Until then, my faithful citizens, LET THE GAMES BEGIN!"

Panic was rising in Pip. It started in her toes and swept up in waves, sloshing against the top of her skull. She was stuck between Lucius and Tiberia, ten rows away from the scene in which her mother was surely going to die.

She dug her fingernails into her palms. Think, think, think, she told herself but the only thoughts that came were grisly ones.

Once Gaius had sat down, the crown began to mumble again. Vendors appeared in the aisles, selling snacks. Men crushed against each other to leave their rows to get food or leave the building to urinate against the palaestra walls. Pip leant forward, her head in her hands.

The herald came back into the arena. He gave three more toots on his bugle, then sprinted back to the iron gates to be let out. The crowd took its seats once more. Pip sat up. At the opposite end of the stadium, she saw a large gate being heaved open. Lucius was overcome by a fit of frenzied clapping. Tiberia slid down in her seat and put her hands over her eyes. She squinted through her fingers at the people entering the arena.

"Oh, you're SUCH a baby," her brother jeered. "They haven't even STARTED yet."

The gladiators entered the ring in two lines, each made up of ten fighters. Two stragglers had to be pushed in by a burly guard standing at the gates. The lines continued to stride through the sand until the fighters were evenly spread out and each man, and one woman, faced their opponent.

The first couple were two very young men, each carrying a short, wooden sword. The second, two fat men covered in oil and wearing strange leather shorts. Pip could see a tall, muscular woman whose fists were bound with leather straps. She faced a shorter boxer, a sickly looking man whose fists were bound in the same way. He was skin and bone, Pip thought. He trembled on stick-thin legs.

Two men carried nets, and craning her neck, Pip could see that the rest of the group were carrying wooden weapons of some sort; sticks or clubs. She hoped Crispus would be fighting with a wooden sword.

The herald returned briefly to the arena. He banged a gong, slipped out again, and the fighting began.

Pip heard a clatter of wood on wood as the sword fighters tested each other. She saw the head of the woman's opponent snap back as she punched him square on the nose. The crowd loved this and cheered its approval.

"She has a left hook just like my wife's," a man yelled from the audience.

The fat oily wrestlers slapped against the wall below Gaius, as each tried to get a good hold on the other's shorts. Pip could hear them grunting and heaving beneath her.

"Daddy, there is no blood," Lucius shouted down to the front. "Daddy, you promised blood." Gaius couldn't hear him.

Pip saw the skill of the fighters as they ducked and dived to avoid being hit. Their sweat was shimmering in the hot sun as they jabbed and prodded with their weapons. She doubted her mum would be this good. She'd only had a few days of training.

A sudden roar erupted from the crowd as the female fighter floored her opponent with a mighty right hook. She pumped her fists in glory as her defeated opponent was dragged unconscious through the sand and out of the black gate by his feet.

The action continued with the other fighters. They displayed great skill, but Lucius was right; there was no bloodshed. The audience started to become restless. Lucius complained.

"This is boring. When are the animals coming on?"

Tiberia had relaxed and was sitting up to watch the swordsmen dance around each other.

"If my little sister likes it, then it MUST be boring," he whined, "BO-RING!"

Exhausted by his tirade, Lucius slumped onto his seat, his chin resting on his chest. A missile whistled past their heads. People from the top tiers had started to throw food into the arena. A low sounding 'boo' began to echo round the walls.

The crowd began to jeer as the two fighters carrying nets stumbled over each other, landing in a tangled heap in the sand. Pip looked down at Lucius. He had fallen asleep. A thin line of purple-tinged slobber ran down his chin.

The herald returned to the arena and banged his gong, signalling for the fighters to stop. Some of them had become engrossed in their bouts and had to be broken up by the guards. The audience jeered and booed as the fighters left.

Suddenly, Marcus came pounding down the stairs. He was followed by the man in the grubby tunic who was supporting a large awning with a tall pole he carried over his head. The other edge of the awning was held up by another man in the next aisle. Pip had an idea,

"Would you like to come with me to meet the gladiators?" she asked Tiberia.

"Really? Oh, yes please, I'd love to."

"The only problem is, I need to free myself of your brother here."

Pip caught Marcus's attention by tugging on the hem of his tunic.

"What is it? Can't you see I'm busy?"

"Did you take wine to the gladiators? Did you take some for your friend Cassius?"

"No, I didn't. I'm far too busy. Spurius hasn't returned yet with the water barrel. I have enough on my plate."

"I can do it for you."

"Do what?"

"Take the gladiators a drink. I'll just need the key so I can undo my chains. Lucius is no bother now since the wine he drank earlier has made him sleepy."

Marcus cast his eyes over to Lucius who was lying unconscious on the stone seat. He delved into his leather pouch. "Alright, but be quick. Make sure Cassius has a good drink and wish him well from me."

Pip caught the keys that Marcus threw before he hurried up the stairs to wait for Spurius. She undid her ankle clasp and tied it around Lucius' free ankle.

"Nip down and get the wine flagon, would you?" she asked Tiberia. "You're small enough to squeeze down the aisles without causing too much bother. Bring it back here, but be careful, it's heavy. Oh, and fetch two goblets."

Tiberia sped away, pleased at being given an important task. She returned a few minutes later, out of breath. She exhaled as she put the heavy flagon down.

"Octavius made a fuss, but Aunty Valentina let me take it for the fighters. She said he'd drunk far too much already."

"Well done. Give it to me and you can carry the goblets. This way, quick." Pip and Tiberia climbed the stairs. They elbowed their way past men swarming on the upper aisle before hurrying down the steps leading to the palaestra. They found themselves outside the gladiators' entrance.

"How will we get in?" Tiberia asked. Pip was about to shrug her shoulders when she saw Ovid's enormous ears bobbing along the path outside the palaestra. Marcus suddenly appeared.

"Thank the Gods for that. Spurius is back."

Spurius' face was a sight to behold. It was crimson, like a tomato.

"If you KNEW the trouble I've had."

"Never mind that now. You're here and that's the main thing."

Marcus leaned into the cart and hauled out the water barrel. He put it down by the gladiators' entrance and banged hard and loud on the door. The door creaked open and the herald's face peeped out,

"Who is it?"

"It's me, you fool. Let me in."

Tiberia and Pip followed Marcus inside. He led them through a dark tunnel, into a cold, damp chamber that smelled of dung. At the far end were animal cages. Pip could see cheetahs lying motionless in one; she saw ostriches in a smaller wooden pen and some wildebeest in a third. Marcus dropped the barrel and instructed the herald to water the animals.

"Where are the gladiators?" Pip asked him.

"Next room along. I need to head back to fix the awning. Gaius was hit in the head with an apple core. If it happens again, Decima will have my guts."

Pip tried not to look at the animals as she passed them. The herald was sloshing water into bowls in the cheetahs' cage but only one seemed interested. Keeping her head down, she passed the ostriches. She heard a voice;

"You're here at last. Your mother will be so relieved."

Pip turned around but couldn't see anybody. She grabbed Tiberia's hand and carried on walking until she felt a sharp peck on the shoulder. She stopped and turned around.

"I'm sorry, I should have introduced myself," one of the ostriches said. "I'm Graham, a friend of Nurse Bladderwash; or I used to be."

"What are you doing here?"

"Who are you talking to?" Tiberia asked.

"Oh, just these giant birds here. Aren't they wonderful? This one is quite friendly. Give him a stroke." Graham bent his head low so Tiberia could touch him. She put down the goblets she was carrying and patted the top of his head. The other ostriches shuffled themselves away to the far side of the pen.

156

"I'm hoping one of the cheetahs will finish me off in the arena, though they don't look too healthy, do they?"

"But why are you here?"

Graham went on, "Unfortunately, I warned a silk merchant about the impending volcano eruption a few years ago. We were talking in the road by his house. He had imported the ostriches for the games that year and I'm sure you know the rest."

"Did you get the years mixed up? Why didn't you come this year, AD 79?"

"Oh, I had a different plan. I wanted an adventure. I wanted to live here for a few years, make a little money, have a little fun."

"Why weren't you killed in the games that year then? The year you were turned into an ostrich."

"Oh, the silk merchant liked to keep a few birds behind to entertain guests at dinner parties. I've been waiting years to have my chance."

"Why are you talking to the bird?" Tiberia started to pull Pip away, "You're scaring me."

"It's alright, Tiberia. I'm coming now. Just give me a minute."

"Anyway, I can help. Your mum told me your plan. I can cause a little trouble in here while you do your thing. Run along now. The little girl is getting spooked."

Pip and Tiberia pressed on into the next chamber. They walked together through the stone arch. The fighters they had seen earlier were laughing and clapping each other on the back near the entrance, having just heard of their impending freedom. Pip nudged her way through them.

It was cool and dark in the underbelly of the amphitheatre. Pip had to narrow her eyes in the gloom, lit only by a few candles scattered around in nooks in the walls. That was when she saw Carrie, her mum. She felt her heart stop beating for a moment. It became a lifeless organ suspended behind her ribs until Tiberia spoke and it pounded back to life,

"There's Cassius," the little girl said, putting down the goblets to tug on Pip's tunic.

Carrie was sitting on a low bench staring at the ground. Cassius sat next to her. He was talking quietly into her ear. Pip could see that Carrie was crying. She put down the flagon of wine and ran over.

"I'm here," she said. They both looked up.

"Ah, the boy who returned my special shield." Cassius rose from the bench. Pip smiled at her mum who held out her hand to touch her face.

"That was Tiberia, really," Pip pulled the little girl towards Cassius. "Tiberia and I have brought some wine for you. We heard all the gladiators were a bit thirsty."

"That's very kind, thank you, but I won't touch wine before a fight. Malefica won't have any either. She's trained very hard. We won't spoil it now."

"Where is Crispus?" Pip asked, "I was told to offer wine to ALL the gladiators."

"He's probably warming up. I should start taking Malefica through some drills too; they're fighting after the animal show. You'll find Crispus three chambers along. All fighters are kept apart from their opponents before a fight. Ask him if he wants some wine. See if you can find Maximus too, if you would," He laughed; "Get him drunk before our fight."

A terrible noise erupted from the animal room. It was an unholy screech the likes of which nobody had heard before. The herald shouted for Cassius to help. Carrie took Tiberia's hand then pulled her close.

Pip quickly turned away and took Decima's silver pot out of the hem of her swimsuit. She poured some wine into a goblet, then mixed the hemlock into it with the silver stirrer.

"Look after Tiberia, would you, Malefica?" she said before leaving the chamber to go and find Crispus.

Pip made her way through the cold dark building, collecting straw and bits of dirt in her sandals as she tried not to spill any of her precious poison. She heard some puffing and panting in a corridor separating two of the chambers.

She peered around the wall. There was Crispus, slicing the air with a heavy iron sword. He swung it around as if it were made of cardboard.

Pip edged around the doorway and coughed but the giant man was in a violent trance.

"Excuse me," she said, but still he grunted and twirled the sword. Pip stepped bravely towards him, holding the goblet high. She could feel the air from the moving weapon rush towards her. Crispus noticed her, stepped back and flung down the sword. It jumped up from the floor and clanged against the wall, inches from her feet.

"I have brought this for you with good wishes from Senator Gaius Ambustus," she said, in awe at the great size of the man, "He wishes you luck. Please drink this to give you strength for your fight." Pip was nervous. Would he believe her?

"Who are you?" Crispus was angry at having been disturbed. His voice was deep and boomed against the walls of the corridor.

"I am the Ambustus house-boy, sir."

"This had better be important. Can't you see that I'm busy?"

"I have brought you a drink of wine from the senator, Mr Crispus, sir." The big man softened. "Why, I haven't tasted wine since before I was captured and forced into slavery."

"I hope you enjoy it, sir; it's for luck. To help you in your fight."

"I don't need luck. Have you seen who I'm fighting? I could beat her with one arm, one eye AND one leg!" He laughed a deep, throaty laugh. "Come closer boy; I won't bite."

Pip crept towards the giant man, holding the goblet out towards him.

"Thank you," he said, reaching down to take it from her. He lifted the wine to his lips and took a sip. Pip held her breath.

"Ah, the sweet fruit of the vines. It plays like music over my tongue. Maybe I should keep it to savour after my fight."

"I wouldn't bother. You'll be a free man after the fight. You can drink as much wine as you like. Did you not hear the decree?"

"I did hear it, yes, but I know that Octavius is a liar. It won't be worth the papyrus it's written on."

"Senator Gaius said to tell you he looks forward to buying you a drink in the tavern after your victory, so it must be true."

"In that case," Crispus held the goblet aloft, "a blessing to Bacchus."

He held the goblet once more to his lips and drained it in one gulp. He put it down gently onto the floor and picked up his sword. He looked deeply into Pip's eyes.

"Thank the senator, would you? I hope to cut Malefica in two for his pleasure."

Twenty

"Don't you kids want to go and see the animal show? I need to start warming Malefica up for her fight."

"Shouldn't you be warming up too? You'll be on soon yourself." Pip was testing the sharpness of the trident Cassius held under his arm with her fingers.

"Don't do that; you'll cut yourself." Carrie pulled Pip's hand away from the spikes and gave it a rub.

"I have to look after my teammate. We're from the same gym, young Pip. We train together, eat and sleep together. Why, sometimes we even die together. But hopefully not today. We have trained hard and we are prepared for every eventuality. Aren't we, Malefica?"

Carrie gave a weak smile.

"Sounds like they're taking the animals to the arena," Pip said. "Poor things."

"I don't want to see the animals being hurt," Tiberia said, burying her face in Carrie's tunic.

"You don't have to. We can stay here until it's over," Pip said, standing up from the bench. She couldn't sit still.

"You should both stay here until the whole thing is over," Carrie was chewing the end of her thumb, "You children shouldn't have to witness any more torment today."

Pip knew what her mum was saying. She didn't want her daughter to see her die.

They heard shouting and goading from the next chamber as the wildebeest reluctantly left their pens.

"They'll let the cheetahs out last. The ostriches are already in,"

Cassius said. "I saw them prancing around when I went to fetch the net and trident. Come on, Malefica, let's get you to the palaestra for some finishing touches. I can't have you going in cold."

"Can I have a few moments with her, please? It won't take long. Fortuna asked me to say a final prayer with her. Is that okay?" asked Pip.

"Two minutes, then send her out. I'll be waiting."

Pip took hold of her mum's hand and pulled her up from the bench. She led her into the corner of the chamber. Carrie rested her forehead on the top of Pip's head.

"You'll be as tall as me in no time," she said trying to stay firm and not cry.

"You'll be with me to see me grow taller when all this is over. Put your hands together as if you're praying." Pip enclosed her mum's hands in hers.

"After you win your fight, and you WILL!" Pip felt the wetness of Carrie's tears as they fell onto her hair, "Don't cry. You'll be fine, I promise. Crispus drank the poisoned wine; in a short while, he'll start to feel the effects and he'll fall like a sack of spuds into the sand. Just wait and see."

Carrie let out a deep sigh.

"Thank you for all you've done, Pip. I am ever so grateful. I am also so very sorry. I am sorry for bringing you here. I had no idea what it would be like. When I die, and that outcome looks pretty likely, you must escape and return home. Toothless isn't so bad, is she?"

"Please don't talk about dying. You must stay positive and fight. You must fight, Mum, with all your heart and then, when you win your freedom, you must find Fortuna.

She has a pink house on the main road into Misenum which is about a four-hour walk from Pompeii. Take the coastal path and head north. I'll see you there after I escape. We will return home together."

"Come on. Now!" Cassius poked his head around the doorway.

"I love you," Carrie said. "Don't ever forget."

"I love you too," whispered Pip and she turned away as her mum left the room.

"Why are you so upset?" Tiberia asked Pip when she returned. "Is Malefica your best friend?"

"She's so much more than that," Pip said, wiping her face with the hem of her tunic. "Do you think they've finished with the animals yet?"

Marcus suddenly burst into the room. He looked cross.

"Here you are. Your mother is worried sick about you, Tiberia. What were you thinking, Pip?"

"I'm sorry, Marcus," Pip quietly sniffed up the remains of her tears. "We brought wine for the gladiators as you asked, then Tiberia said she was worried about seeing the animals hurt, so we were just going to stay here for a while."

"Gaius and Decima want their daughter with them for the rest of the show. Lucius has already wormed his way back to the front row. Where did you put the keys, by the way? He's still in his chains."

"Didn't I give them back to you? I'm sure I did," Pip lied.

"Oh, maybe. I've been very busy. I must have mislaid them. Oh well, it won't do him any harm."

"What about the animals?" Tiberia asked.

"Don't worry, that's all over. A bit of a damp squib really. The crowd are throwing things again. I hope the Malefica fight wins them over or there'll be a stampede."

"Are all the animals dead?"

"No, they're not. A very strange thing happened. The wildebeest were out, huddled in a corner, terrified, poor things. The ostriches had scattered all around the arena, apart from one which practically offered its neck to the only cheetah we managed to get in there. The cheetah killed it instantly but then a very odd thing happened. A man appeared on the arena floor just where the ostrich had died. He came behind the cheetah, put it in a headlock until it passed out, then calmly walked out of the arena. Just like that. I have no idea where he came from. Maybe Gaius had arranged for him to be made an example of. He was probably a criminal; a murderer maybe."

"What happened next?" Tiberia asked.

"Nothing really. With the cheetah out of action, the wildebeest and the other ostriches will live to see another day. Gaius asked me if the amateur gladiators from earlier might be made to go back in and finish everything off with spears, but they've all scarpered, having been freed. Anyway, you two, back to your seats. I'll take you up myself."

Marcus bent low to pick Tiberia up. Pip wondered about making a run for it, but Marcus' giant hand clamped onto her shoulder and grabbed a handful of her tunic. With this, he steered her ahead of him, through the dark chambers and out of the palaestra door. They passed Carrie just as she was practising throwing her net over Cassius.

"That's good, very good. Remember, though, Crispus is much taller than me so you need to throw it just that little bit higher." Cassius noticed Marcus walking past; "Just putting the icing on the cake," he shouted over.

"Good luck for your fight, brother, I'll see you after for a drink," Marcus called out as he ushered Pip up the stairs.

Inside the amphitheatre, the audience had taken to the aisles again. The atmosphere seemed to have changed. There was a menacing feeling, a disgruntled hum in the air.

"Get out of my way," Marcus yelled, pushing past a group of men who were playfighting on the steps.

"Shut your face or I'll knock your teeth out," the smallest of them said, standing wide to bar his way. Marcus let go of Pip's tunic and put Tiberia down gently. He grabbed the man around the neck.

"Alright, alright, calm down," one of the other men said. "He didn't mean it."

Marcus let go of the man who had to catch his breath, and took hold of Tiberia's hand,

"Quickly, you two, down to the front," he said, barging his way through a sea of bodies until the three of them were at the family's aisle.

"There she is. Where have you been, darling?" Decima shouted over when she caught sight of her daughter. "I thought you'd been eaten by a lion. Leave that slave boy and come and sit next to me."

"But I want to stay with Pip."

"Get rid of the boy, would you, Marcus?" Gaius turned his head to speak. "There's a chap."

"I won't sit with you unless Pip can sit with me. I won't!" Tiberia stamped her foot.

"Oh, very well. I'm sorry Octavius, Valentina, would you mind shifting along so they can get by? Can you make a little room, Remus? Thank you so much."

So there Pip found herself, sitting on the front row of the gladiatorial games, in Pompeii in AD79, with the senator, his wife and Tiberia on her left and Lucius on her right. She was trapped. She was trapped and about to watch her mother take on a gladiator with over fifty scalps. Lucius elbowed her in the ribs.

"Where did you get to? You left me all by myself. Did you take my sister to see Cassius?"

Pip looked down and noticed Lucius' chained legs. She couldn't help smiling.

"It's NOT funny. I'm going to get you later; you wait and see."

"You'll have to catch me first. I don't fancy your chances."

The bickering stopped when the herald entered the arena. He gave three blasts on his bugle. The crowd shuffled back to its seats. When it was quiet, the herald shouted out,

"Men of Pompeii, I give you Crispus and Malefica."

The gates on the left side of the arena creaked open. The crowd held its breath. Pip chewed the insides of her cheeks until she tasted blood. Carrie took five steps into the arena. She stopped briefly and looked up into the sun. Pip thought how small she looked, and how unprotected, wearing only an arm guard. In her left hand, she held her net, in her right, the trident.

She continued walking until she faced Gaius from the middle of the arena. The crowd jeered and whistled. She stopped and gave a short bow. Gaius nodded his head and clapped. He turned aside to his wife, saying,

"She's got a cat in hell's chance."

The other gate then creaked open. The crowd erupted when Crispus strode out. Recognisable only by the fact he was missing an arm, he wore a rounded helmet with tiny holes to see out of and he wore a large rectangular shield over his body, like a tabard.

"I don't see how that's fair," Pip said to nobody in particular.

"Who cares about fair?" Lucius piped up. "Anyway, Crispus is a secutor. He'll want a quick finish, otherwise, he will tire. All that armour makes him tired, especially in the hot sun. Malefica is a net-man, well, a net-woman. Net-men rely on agility and speed to harm their opponents. Nobody cares much about net-men though. They really are the lowest of the low. Crispus will end her in seconds."

"Then why doesn't a secutor face another secutor? Wouldn't that be fairer?" Pip had to shout above the din as Crispus advanced to the centre of the arena.

"Who cares about fair? Come on, Crispus!" Lucius yelled. "Slay the thief!"

Crispus stopped a short distance away from Carrie. He also turned to Gaius and bowed. The senator again nodded his head. He gave a small smile. The herald returned to give one more blast on his bugle. The fight had begun.

Pip noticed that two guardsmen had slipped in and were standing, one in front of each of the big gates. They each held a wooden cudgel. They were a warning to Pip's mum that running away was futile.

A hasty chill passed over Pip as the sun became eclipsed by a thick sheet of cloud. Her mum's tiny figure no longer cast a meagre shadow in the sand. The crowd started to boo. Tentatively, Carrie jabbed her trident into the air towards Crispus. The big man roared with laughter.

"I TOLD you she was plucky," Octavius became animated. "Skewer him, Malefica!"

Crispus advanced towards Carrie, his entire torso protected by the rectangular shield. He let his sword dangle by his left side.

"Come on, woman!" he bellowed to her, "let's give them what they came for!"

Pip wondered when the hemlock would begin to take effect. It must be well over an hour since Crispus had drunk the wine. He was such a big man. What if Fortuna had got the dosage wrong?

Crispus suddenly raised his sword and jabbed it towards Carrie who easily dodged it. She thrust her trident forward to gauge distance, just as Cassius had taught her. It made a thud on Crispus' armour.

This is hopeless, Pip thought. She doesn't stand a chance. Crispus is covered from head to toe. Or is he? Pip noticed that he only wore armour on his right leg. Just as she had noticed this, Carrie danced round to the back of Crispus and dug her trident into his exposed calf.

Crispus looked shocked and lost his balance for a moment. Shamed by the blow, he gave a roar and charged at Carrie with his sword aimed at her chest. Carrie immediately dodged the attack, stepping deftly away.

"What's wrong with him?" Lucius whined. "Why doesn't he just chop her head off?"

Heartened by success, Carrie swung her trident at Crispus' helmet. Apart from making a loud clang, the blow had no effect at all. She tried again and Crispus swatted the trident away as if it was a matchstick. Carrie lost her grip on the wooden shaft and it fell to the floor.

"That's it now! She's finished!" Lucius yelled. Tiberia hid her face in the crook of her arm.

Undeterred, Carrie slipped behind Crispus. As he turned to face her, she hooked her foot around his ankle, shoved his chest, and swept him off his feet. Both he and his sword clattered to the ground. Carrie rushed to pick her trident up. By the time she had it in her hands again, Crispus had hauled himself to his feet. He bent low to collect his sword. He seemed to be moving slowly now.

"She's going to grind him down, clever girl!" Octavius cheered.

Carrie danced behind the big man again and sunk the trident into the back of his leg. Crispus dropped his sword, shocked by the searing pain. The crowd roared. Carrie looked up and smiled, her pride blinding her to Crispus' armoured arm, being swung at her head like a club. She saw stars and fell down heavily into the sand.

"That's it, finish her off," Lucius yelled.

Crispus had to bend low again to retrieve his sword. Carrie forced herself to come to, and scrabbled over the arena floor until she was able to wrap her hands around Crispus' feet. She held them tight and pushed his shins with her head. Crispus fell backwards like a marble statue.

167

Again, the crowd roared but something strange had happened. A sharp wind had picked up and the light had turned very low. Pip saw her mum shudder as a tremor passed under her feet. The crowd began to mutter.

Crispus heaved himself to his knees and picked up his sword. Having only one arm was proving difficult for him. He dug his sword into the trembling sand and tried to lever himself up. Carrie took her chance and threw her net over him, then she kicked him to the floor.

A deep rumble shook the ground. Carrie widened her stance to keep her balance. A second rumble followed. Octavius yelped from the front row,

"Finish him off, Malefica! Take his sword and finish him off! What are you waiting for?"

Carrie looked down at her opponent. He had rolled onto his back. He was motionless. She knelt down and tugged his helmet off through the net. It made a sucking noise as it popped over his head. Crispus' eyes were closed. He was fast asleep.

Carrie put one foot on Crispus' chest and made a victory salute, but the crowd had stopped paying attention to the fight. A third louder rumble had sent the higher tiers of the audience running for the exits. Carrie noticed that the awning had collapsed over the family on the front seats. The ground began to violently shake. The stone structure of the amphitheatre was strong, but the wooden staircases were splitting.

Carrie left Crispus in the sand, and, lurching and reeling over the rolling ground, made her way over to the small black door. Under the darkness of the fallen awning, Pip couldn't see her mother go through the door to her freedom.

Twenty-One

"Pass the olive oil, would you, darling? Thank you." Gaius slopped dressing over his salad then sighed, "The most disastrous games in history. I'm a laughing stock."

"It wasn't your fault there was an earthquake. These things are in the hands of the gods." Decima reached out and touched her husband's hand.

"Maybe we didn't pray enough. Maybe we angered them in some way. I don't understand it. We make regular offerings to Bacchus."

"In future, we will by-pass him and pray directly to Jupiter. Next year, darling, I'm sure you'll be re-elected. Then, when you have another chance to host the games, they'll be spectacular, I promise."

"It wasn't just the earthquake was it though, dear heart? It was a disaster from start to finish."

"I can't help thinking Marcus didn't quite pull his weight. I told him so in the cart on the way home. He made me get in with the children in case the earth swallowed us up. Such an indignity, being pulled along like a sack of grain by a miniature donkey. But I told him I thought he'd been lazy. I let him have it."

"I hope you didn't, darling. He'll be awfully cross. He's rather sensitive at the moment. I don't know what's wrong with him. Look, here come the children."

Lucius made his way slowly to the dining table, dragging his chains behind him.

"Why is my son still in chains? It's a bloody disgrace. Why hasn't Marcus seen to it? Lucius is the senator's son, for the love of the Gods."

"He didn't come home last night. He had business to finish off at the amphitheatre." Gaius stood up and lifted Tiberia onto a bench. She was chattering excitedly.

"Cassius gave me his shield, Daddy, but I'm going to give it to Pip, our slave boy."

"Over my dead body!" Lucius heaved himself onto the bench beside her. His chains clanked against the stone.

"Cassius gave his shield to me and I may do with it what I like."

"Don't be silly, darling. Slaves can't own property. Lucius would appreciate it more than a feeble-minded slave anyway. Lucius simply adores Cassius, don't you, my love?" Decima passed a plate of cheese towards the children.

"Cassius was lucky to have been granted his freedom without even having to fight," said Gaius as he rubbed his chin. "I'm surprised he took his liberty, to be honest. Fighting was his life. Maybe he'll be back. Some of them can't handle life as a citizen."

"Yes, and when he comes back to fight again, he'll take the shield back from you." Lucius pinched Tiberia hard on the inside of her arm. The bit that really hurts. She slapped him away.

"I am going to give the shield to Pip. So there!"

"And you say Crispus woke up in the chambers after they dragged him out?" Decima popped a piece of tomato into her mouth.

"Yes. Everyone thought his heart had stopped. Malefica did terrifically well, dancing around him as she did. She showed great heart before the earth began to shake.

Here's Marcus now." Gaius stood up to make room on his bench. "Come and join us for a spot of lunch, would you?" Marcus had a large papyrus scroll under his arm.

"I have something I need to talk to you about," he said. "I'd prefer to stand."

"Oh, not now." Decima puffed out her cheeks. "Can't you see we're having a nice family lunch? And will you take those wretched chains from my son's ankles?""

"I will see to that later, Madam. This will not wait, I'm afraid. It's very important."

"Very well," Gaius said, "but make it quick. There's a good chap."

Pip came rushing into the garden.

"Excuse me, Master Gaius, Spurius asked me to let you know that the slaughterman has arrived."

"What's that funny smell?" Lucius was kicking his heels and making his chains clank against the stone bench.

"Stop being mean to Pip. He doesn't smell as bad as you."

"No, really. There's a funny smell. Can you smell it, Mummy?"

Decima pointed her nose in the air. "Yes, I think I can, sweetheart. I think I can smell smoke."

"Someone's probably burning farm rubbish on the hills," Gaius said. "Let's get the mule out of the way, shall we, Marcus?"

"No, truly, Master, there's something very important I have to say to you."

"Here's Varius now. Be a good chap and take him to the stable, would you?"

A tall thin man appeared in the garden. He carried a leather tool bag. Tiberia jumped down from her bench and ran out of the dining room towards him. Marcus caught her by her tunic.

"I won't let him do it, I won't!" she howled. Marcus held her under one arm as she tried to wriggle free.

"He's a good slaughterman, Tiberia. It will be quick," Marcus tried to soothe the little girl who was now sobbing and gulping into his chest.

Gaius was left to greet Varius.

"Good afternoon. I'm sorry about the disturbance. My youngest became rather attached to the old beast. Come this way."

Gaius led Varius to the stable and unbolted the door. "There's two in there. Make sure you dispatch the right one. We're keeping the little fellow."

Gaius ushered the slaughterman into the stable and shut the door behind him.

Back at the table, Marcus had lifted Tiberia back onto her bench and knelt down so he could speak to her gently,

"It will be over very soon. Dentata had a good life and she knows you loved her very much. It won't hurt. She won't feel a thing and remember, little Ovid needs a good friend now." Tiberia was too upset to speak.

Suddenly, a violent scream split the air. The stable door swung open. Varius sped out and ran across the garden, not stopping to pick up the tools that were spilling out of his bag.

With Marcus distracted, Tiberia managed to break free from his grasp and run to the stable.

"Come back, Tiberia," Decima shouted, clutching her necklace. "Lucius, you go with her. She's upset."

"No," Marcus said, "Pip, you go and see that she's alright."

"I don't want my daughter in all that mess; that's a clean tunic."

"It's good that she learns the circle of life," Gaius said. "Let her say goodbye. Now, can you please pass the bread?"

Pip followed Tiberia into the stable and closed the door. She found her standing behind Ovid, staring at the stable floor. Pip gently nudged the mule out of her way.

Sitting cross-legged, holding a blanket around herself, was Jane Jones. She held a hand out to Tiberia;

"Please don't be afraid. I am Dentata, your old friend. I am just in a different form, that's all."

"No, you're not. Dentata was a mule. What have you done with her?"

"When the slaughterman cut my throat, I turned back into a human. My name is Jane. I was a human many years ago and was turned into a mule because I was naughty and broke some rules. Being turned into a mule was my punishment."

"But how? What rules?" Tiberia had stopped crying but her face remained red and bloated.

"I can't really explain. It's just magic."

"Why should I believe you? How do I know you're not making it all up?"

"Do you remember when Lucius stole your apple and I bit his bottom? Do you remember bringing me bread from the kitchen all those times and I would always lick your hand as a thank you? Do you remember hiding behind my fat tummy when Lucius was looking for you? And look, I still have the braid you put in my hair."

Tiberia bent down and touched the green ribbon she'd plaited into Dentata's mane. Jane grabbed her hands.

"My darling girl, I want to thank you for being so kind to me for all those years. It's not easy being a mule and you made life so much more bearable for me. I cannot thank you enough. I want you to be strong and grow up to be a strong young woman. Don't ever let that horrible brother of yours let you feel that you're anything less than wonderful."

Jane heaved herself up and folded Tiberia up in her arms. Reluctantly, and with a sigh, after a few moments, she pulled away.

"I need to escape now before the family find me and have me arrested. Ovid is here though, and he will need you to be kind to him in the same way you were kind to me."

Tiberia ran her hand down Ovid's back and put her arms around his neck.

"That's it. He's a cute little chap. He's far prettier than I was." Jane stood up. Pip helped her tie the blanket around herself with some twine.

"I have to leave now. Goodbye, Tiberia, and thank you."

Pip led Tiberia back to the table by her hand.

"There's my girl. Not so bad after all, eh?" Gaius picked Tiberia up and placed her back on the bench. She gave a weak smile.

"What happened with Varius? Why did he go running off like a headless chicken?"

"Dentata didn't make it easy for him, Master Gaius. She gave him a hard nip before he could kill her," Pip said, "but he returned while we were there to take the body out of the back door."

"Very good. She could be a spiteful old mule and that's the truth. Anyway, boy, you certainly have a way with young Tiberia here. What's your name?"

"His name is Pip, Master Gaius, as I have told you before on many occasions. Now, can I please have your full attention?"

Marcus stepped forward, holding onto the scroll.

"Go on then. What is it that's bothering you?"

"I have a proposition for you. Well, it's more of an ultimatum."

"Let's hear it," Gaius looked attentive suddenly.

"I can smell smoke," Lucius piped up. "In fact, I can SEE smoke."

"Hush, please, Marcus is talking," Gaius said.

"He's right, darling." Decima could see a waft of smoke curling around Bacchus' statue. "And I don't see why whatever Marcus has to say is so important. Can't he discuss it in the office with you later?"

"With respect, Madam Decima, I want to talk to Gaius now. This won't wait another minute."

"Go on, Marcus, I'm listening."

"I want my freedom, Master. In fact, I want my freedom, Quinta's freedom and I want the freedom of all the other slaves you own. We will continue to work for you, for a decent wage but we must all do it as freed people."

"Well, steady on now!" Gaius was shocked.

"I've never heard anything so preposterous in my life," said Decima who seemed to have lost control of the lower half of her face. Her jaw had become slack with disbelief.

"Slaves are also human beings, Master. We have feelings just like you. We have hopes and we have dreams. We are not animals."

"All slaves are animals," Lucius sang, "Piggy, piggy animals."

"We are NOT animals, Master, and without us, forgive my bluntness, without us, you would be nothing."

A large crack sounded in the distance and a rumble travelled across the paving stones in the garden.

"Make it stop, Daddy, I'm scared." Tiberia left her bench and made her way to her father's lap. Gaius stopped her from climbing up. He held her away from him.

"I don't like what you're saying, Marcus. I have built this business up with hard work, discipline and intelligence."

"With respect, sir, you inherited the business from your father."

"With RESPECT, Marcus," Gaius spat the words out, "with RESPECT, the fish sauce business I inherited from my father, may

174

the Gods rest his soul, when passed over to me, was on its knees. Look at it now. My sauce is famous throughout the world."

"Again, with RESPECT, Master Gaius, without me, your business would still be on its knees. I have carried you, and it, for many years. Your input has been minimal. I do everything for you whilst you swan about in your robes, taking all the credit. It has been MY hard work, MY discipline and MY intelligence that has made it a success, not to mention the hard labour of the men you have cooped up in the factory all day."

"I am sorry," Decima stood up, "but I won't have you speaking to my husband in this way."

A sharp earth tremor sent Decima falling back onto the bench. The single curl of smoke had been joined by several others. The smoke passed over the dining table and made the children cough.

Marcus was undeterred and carried on;

"I have a scroll here that names all of the slaves you own. I have spoken with a lawyer and drawn up a contract for every one of us. We will all be granted our freedom but guarantee that we will continue to work for you, in the same manner, for the continuation of your profitable business, for the rest of our working lives. We want a living wage. I would like you to sign every scroll."

"And if I refuse?"

"And refuse you WILL. You will sign those scrolls over my dead body." Decima began to cough. She covered her face with her hands. "Look what Octavius has started with all his 'freeing slaves' nonsense. It's ludicrous."

"I think we need to leave," Gaius said. "The smoke is too much. Something bad is happening. We will talk about this later."

"We will talk about it NOW, Master Gaius. Here is the wax; you are wearing your official ring. Please sign the scrolls now. If you refuse, then Quinta and I have no choice but to leave. We will leave Rome altogether if we have to. We MUST have our freedom."

The ground shuddered and sent Bacchus crashing to the ground. His head snapped off and rolled along the garden, resting at Gaius' sandalled feet. Tiberia and Lucius started to scream. Marcus held a flame under a small block of red wax.

"Sign them please, Gaius."

"This is ridiculous. My husband will have you flogged and thrown in jail. You need us. You cannot survive without us. We OWN you, for Jupiter's sake."

Marcus ignored Decima.

"Sign the scrolls."

Just as Gaius pressed his ring into the wax on the final document, a cloud of ash passed the sun and the garden darkened.

"Thank you, Gaius, you won't regret it. Now, I think we must all get indoors. It looks like the world is about to end."

The family made its way into the house as the garden walls began to split and crack. They tumbled through the corridor and assembled in the hall. Stones were collecting in the pool by the shrine.

Quinta came running down the stairs and fell into Marcus' arms.

"What's happening?" she asked. "Is there another earth tremor?"

"I think it's far worse than that," Marcus said. "Go and get Spurius from the kitchen. He's probably napping. That man can sleep through anything. Everyone must stay here. I'll be back as soon as I can," he commanded before running over the dog mosaic and out into the street.

Decima swooned with fear, so Gaius laid her on a couch, above which a painting swayed precariously. He sat beside her, cradling her head in his hands.

"Lucius, take your sister's hand. Look after her," he said, but his son was rigid with fear. Tiberia took his hand instead.

Quinta had found Spurius on the floor beneath his pans in the kitchen. He was bleeding from a wound on his head. Pip helped her drag him into the hall.

Marcus returned, saying,

"We need to get away, Master. All the houses in town are falling apart. There are people swarming in the street. The air is turning grey and it's thick with soot. We can take the fishing boat and leave by sea. Thank the Gods we still have Ovid and the cart is still in one piece.

Quinta, help the children and Decima gather up some essentials. I'll start making space in the cart."

Quinta had to grab Decima's wrist and haul her up from the couch. She pulled her towards the bedrooms. Tiberia did the same with Lucius.

"HURRY UP!" Marcus shouted after them.

Spurius had come to and was rubbing his head.

"Are you alright, my friend?" Marcus asked. The cook nodded. "Good, there's no time to lose. Go and fetch some food and water from the kitchen. Pip, go and help."

Another violent tremor sent the shrine crashing to the floor. Gaius jumped up, terrified.

"For the love of Bacchus, Marcus. What's happening? Are we all going to die?"

"I don't know, Master. We have a chance but only if we act quickly. Look, here comes Decima and the children. Let's get them into the cart."

Gaius crossed the hall to help his family over the rubble. He stopped dead when he saw what his wife was holding in her arms.

"What in the name of Jupiter have you got there? Marcus told you to fetch essentials only!"

"Oh, what does HE know? He's a slave, darling. Or he was. Either way, he's an unrefined dolt. I absolutely refuse to leave my new gown behind and, of course, I am not going anywhere without my mirror."

"The city is crashing down around our ears, Decima; see sense, PLEASE!"

"No, I am not going anywhere without my nice things." She flung herself back down on the couch.

Exasperated, he turned to the children. Lucius held a pile of clothes and some toys. He limped awkwardly in his chains. Tiberia had her arms full with the shield Cassius had given her.

"Gods preserve us. What in the name of Hades have you got that thing for?"

"It will protect us from the falling stones."

"She has a point, Master," Marcus said, taking the heavy shield from her. "Come on, let's get you into the cart."

177

Pip and Spurius returned from the kitchen carrying some bread and a large jar of water.

"Did you bring wine?" Decima asked.

"Darling, PLEASE," Gaius reasoned, but his wife wasn't listening. She snatched the water jar from Spurius and crunched determinedly through the broken bits of masonry and pottery until she'd made it to the kitchen.

"There," she declared on her return. "A small libation for the journey. I suggest we make for Naples. My mother will be so pleased to see us all."

Marcus sighed,

"Pip, can you fetch Ovid from the stable? Go via the front door."

She did as she was told, leaping over the dog mosaic which had split in two. A crack had appeared down the middle of its red tongue. She left the house and went to fetch the mule who was still safe in his stable.

There was less time between tremors now; they came quickly and more violently. Pip led Ovid to the front of the house, steadying herself after the latest vibration. She was pleased the family were heading for Naples. Misenum and her mother were not too far along the coast.

She searched in the gloom for the outline of the cart and led Ovid to the front of the vehicle. The mule backed himself obligingly between the shafts and Pip buckled up his harness. She shielded her face from the torrents of stones with her arm. The mule hung his head low to avoid the blows. He stamped his feet and snorted.

Pip heard the family as they jostled with each other trying to get out of the house.

"There are stones raining from the sky, Gaius. I can't possibly come out. My hair will be spoiled." Decima had lagged behind.

"Go and fetch your wife, Gaius," Marcus ordered. "I will get the children." He held an oil lamp aloft. The air was thick with ash and dust. Tiberia began to cry as Marcus lifted her up and into the cart.

"Lucius, come and sit beside your sister. Hold the shield over her." Marcus had to lift Lucius into the cart as he couldn't jump in his chains. "Squeeze yourselves into the back, that's it; now, where's your mother?"

Gaius had hold of Decima around her waist. He lifted her towards the cart as she kicked and struggled.

"My gown! I have dropped it. Let GO of me!"

"Here, let me help her up." Marcus took hold of Decima and launched her towards the children.

"Be careful, you great oaf," she whined as she fell roughly against Lucius.

"Oh, do be quiet," Gaius said. "Marcus, get the boy in the cart and I'll help Spurius up; I think he's still a bit dazed. I can help you lead the mule."

"Where is Quinta?" Decima shouted, "I need her here. I can barely breathe."

"I'm here, madam," she called through the gloom. She had hold of Decima's gown. "I'm just hopping up."

"Is that everyone?" asked Gaius, "Right-o then. Giddy up."

The wheels of the cart squeaked under the weight of the family as Ovid slowly eased it away from the house. As the mule raised his head, a shower of stones pelted his face. Marcus tried to shield him as best as he could.

"I can't breathe," Decima complained again. "Help me, Gaius, please. I think I'm dying."

Thinking quickly, Quinta picked up Decima's gown from the bottom of the cart and began to tear it up.

"What in Jupiter's name are you DOING? Have you gone mad?" Decima reached out to snatch the gown but lost her balance and fell into a heap. Quinta continued to tear the gown into seven lengths of cloth. She handed them out to everyone.

"Here, cover your mouths with these," she directed.

Larger stones were falling now. Every so often, Ovid would whinny in pain as one hit him on the head, or he'd flick his tail when one struck his back. Still, bravely, he pulled the cart towards the harbour.

The cart lurched as Ovid stumbled over a fallen stone. The children shrieked. A stone hit Spurius on the back of his neck making him cry out.

"This is useless. We'll never make it. We're on a cart ride to Hades."

"It's not far now," Marcus shouted back towards his friend. "Let's all try and stay calm."

They turned a corner onto the main road. Pip could see shadowy figures running this way and that. Some were wailing, some silent. People were crouching in shop doorways, huddled together for comfort. Dogs were straining at their leashes, tethered to their spots. This is it, she thought. This is really it.

"The end of the world has come upon us!" a man shouted through the murk, his arms raised to the sky. A rock landed on his head and he fell down. Pip put her face back into the crook of her arm, not wanting to see.

Still, the cart rolled on. The children cried muffled sobs into their makeshift hankies. Decima had discarded hers, preferring to glug wine from her jug. She was still angry about her torn and ruined gown.

As they approached the city walls, the crowds got thicker. People were streaming out of the town, holding on tightly to their possessions and onto the frailer members of their families. Everyone was coughing.

Visibility was poor and stones kept raining down. Screams and bawling filled the air. Arguments about leaving or staying could be heard through open doors. Some thought the chaos would pass, others that Pompeii was doomed and should be abandoned.

Ovid was stumbling now. Marcus held tightly to his harness and said words of encouragement into his floppy ears.

Suddenly, a tiny voice rang out from the shadows;

"Gaius is that you? It's your friend Stephanus. I have Valentina here. Can you help us? We have nowhere to go."

"Of course, my good man," Gaius replied, coughing, "We have a boat for Naples. And Valentina, I'm sure there's room for all of us. Where is Octavius?"

"Oh, he wouldn't leave his vines," she spluttered. "Let him perish with his blessed grapes."

Quinta jumped out of the cart and gave Valentina and Crispus a piece of cloth each.

"Here, take these; put them over your mouths." She took hold of Valentina's arm and guided her alongside the cart.

"We must press on," Marcus wheezed, "I can see the harbour walls."

A bottleneck had formed at the sea gate, with fleeing people forcing themselves through the narrow entrance. People were teeming around the cart, pushing and shoving.

"Everybody get out. The cart is a hindrance. We can leave it behind now," Marcus said. He left Gaius with Ovid and started to help the others down from the cart.

"I want everyone to hold hands. That's right, in a chain. It's easy to get lost in this gloom.

"What about Ovid?" Tiberia suddenly shouted.

"We don't need him now, darling," Gaius said.

"We can't leave him behind; he'll die."

"Don't be silly, Tiberia. We can get another one in Naples," said Decima.

"Ovid tried his hardest to get us here safely, and you're just going to abandon him. You are cruel, Mummy. If Ovid is staying, then I am too." Tiberia broke the chain of hands and ran back to the mule. She undid his harness and led him away from the cart.

Marcus followed her, saying,

"It's alright. We will bring him. We can't leave the little fella to die. Get in line. I will hold his reins."

It took a long time for the family to reach the sea. Marcus led with Ovid, while the rest formed a chain from behind. Tiberia was first, holding onto the mule's tail. They made their way like this as hundreds of people swarmed around, dazed by the smog and hurt by falling rocks. Fights broke out by the harbour as people clamoured to get onto boats that didn't belong to them.

At the harbour, Marcus paused.

"Pip, take hold of Ovid's reins. Everyone else, form a tight huddle. I am going to prepare the boat." Pip pulled Ovid's face into her tunic to protect him from the soot. A few moments later, Marcus returned.

"The boat is ready. Cassius was on board. He has Crispus with him."

"Oh, how wonderful," Decima complained, "a one-armed oarsman."

"You are welcome to row in his place," Marcus said. "And you should be grateful to Crispus; he managed to see off a rabble of men who were trying to steal the boat. They are bringing it around to us."

The harbour wall was high.

"Throw up a rope," Marcus shouted. He tied it to an iron ring on the quayside.

"Children first!" Marcus clutched the rope and scaled the wall backwards. Holding onto the rope with one arm, he scooped the other around Tiberia's waist.

"Put your arms around my neck; that's it." Marcus climbed down the rope until his feet reached the bottom of the boat. He repeated this with Lucius, Decima and Valentina. Pip and Quinta were able to climb down the rope themselves. Spurius lost his grip on the rope and landed heavily, making the boat rock from side to side. Stephanus fell into the water and had to be fished out by Cassius. Gaius came last.

"Ovid!" Tiberia cried.

"Oh, just leave him; stop making a fuss," Decima pleaded. Marcus looked at his hands; they were red and sore and rope-burned. He then looked at Tiberia's sad face and he climbed up the rope once more.

"Throw me another rope," he called out to Cassius when he reached the quayside. He returned exhausted, but with the mule tied to his back. The rope had cut into his neck.

"Take him off me, would you? He's heavy." Spurius jumped up to untie him.

"Where are all our things?" Decima asked. "Everything has been left behind. We have nothing. How can we survive without our THINGS?"

"We have life, Madam Decima. We have life and we have family and we have friends. Most importantly, we have our freedom. Now, Gaius, Crispus, Cassius, have you each got an oar? Let me take the fourth."

Decima and Valentina both crouched at the bow of the boat. Quinta took Stephanus and the children to the stern and there they huddled together amongst the fishing nets and lobster creels. To make room for Ovid, Pip sat at the edge of the boat, her feet hanging over the edge.

The boat set off shakily until the men found their rhythm. Soon, the soot and smoke cleared and the lights of Naples appeared, glinting in the distance. Lucius and Tiberia cheered. Pip slipped silently into the water.

Twenty-Two

"I think she looks great in her school uniform."

Pip was standing on a chair in the big kitchen. Carrie had pins in her mouth and was fiddling with the hem of Pip's skirt. She took the pins out to reply;

"Yes, she does. I'm pleased she's going to school at last. She's missed so much. Thankfully, she had you to teach her to read at least."

Harriet Higgins was fussing with a ladder she'd found in her tights.

"I wonder if I'll ever get used to these things again."

She took another biscuit from the plate on the table by the hearth, basking in the glow of a roaring fire. She gave a custard cream a nibble before speaking.

"I learned a lot from her too, you know. She was a tonic for a poor old mouse like me. And of course, I had made you a promise. I'm so proud of her, rescuing you like that. She's a very brave young woman."

There was a loud knock on the door. Jane came racing into the kitchen, books stuffed under one arm.

"I'll get it. Oh, hello, Sergeant Bunn, do come in."

Pip jumped off her chair to greet Lester. She sat down on the stone floor and he jumped all over her, licking her face,

"Oh, Pip, you'll spoil your uniform. Stop it, Lester; come to heel."

"Can I offer you a cup of tea, Sergeant?" Carrie asked. "There are cakes in the pantry."

"Did I hear someone say tea?" Graham had appeared at the front door looking dishevelled. "It's thirsty work painting the locks. I hope they'll be ready in time for the grand opening next week."

"Hello, Graham," the policeman said, "and yes, please, I'd love a cup of tea. I have some good news for Carrie and young Pip."

"Sit down at the table then. Graham can put the kettle on." Carrie put her pins back in her sewing basket. "What is your news? Graham, can you fetch the Battenburg?"

"Toothless and Nurse Bladderwash will be standing trial at the Old Bailey next week. I expect the judge to put them away for an eternity. The list of charges is as long as my arm. And Carrie, with Toothless safely in gaol, and with Mrs Higgins waiving her succession, as you are the next in line to the Nash fortune, you, my dear, will inherit the lot."

"You mean Pip and I will get to stay in this house?"

"It's your house now and that's not all. We found a safe under the floorboards. There are oodles of things inside; jewels, gold, all sorts. Because we can't tell what belonged to old Nash and what was procured illegally by Toothless and Bladderwash, it will all go to you."

"That's great news!" Jane slapped the table hard. "What do you say, Pip?"

"It is good news, yes. I'm just glad to be home and to have my mum back. Thank you, Mrs Higgins. You have been very kind."

Carrie got up and moved to the back of Pip's chair. She leaned over and held her tightly.

"And I am over the moon to be here with you."

"Can someone please bring me a slice of cake," Mrs Higgins called over. "I can't survive on crumbs anymore. I'm making up for lost time."

"Can I get you another cup of tea, Sergeant?" Carrie asked, taking a slice of cake over to the fireplace.

"No, thank you," the policeman said getting up. "I have to get back to work. I just popped in to share my news."

"Thank you," Pip said, getting up to give Lester a goodbye pat.

After the policeman had left, Carrie turned to Pip;

"I think you should have an early night. You have a big day tomorrow."

"I think school will be a breeze after the week I've had."

Carrie laughed.

"You might be right. Goodnight, Pip. I'll see you in the morning."

Lightning Source UK Ltd.
Milton Keynes UK
UKHW020112070422
401169UK00007B/190

9 781802 273571